Mama, Can Giraffes
Life lessons from a Giraffe
Volume 3

Written and illustrated by
Tasha Poochette

Mama, Can Giraffes Talk? Life lessons from a Giraffe
Volume 3

Cover design, texts and illustrations by Tasha Poochette

Copyright © 2018 Tasha Poochette
All rights reserved.
May not be reproduced or distributed without consent.

Published by Tasha Poochette
ISBN-13: 978-1718902312
ISBN-10: 171890231X

I was lucky enough to have a "Summer" for a mother. Thanks Mama for all the life lessons you taught me. This book, like my first two books, is dedicated to you. I also want to thank my family and friends, who provided valuable input and encouraged me to keep writing about Baby G's journey.

Table of Contents

Baby G: Mama, what is magic? .... - 1 -
Baby G: Mama, what is a community? .... - 6 -
Baby G: Mama, what are traditions? .... - 9 -
Baby G: Mama, what are Christmas carols? .... - 12 -
Baby G: Mama, what are servants? .... - 15 -
Baby G: Mama, what does "follow your heart" mean? .... - 17 -
Baby G: Mama, what is a snow day? .... - 18 -
Baby G: Mama, what does "better late than never" mean? .... - 20 -
Baby G: Mama, what are directions? .... - 23 -
Baby G: Mama, what is a spectacle? .... - 25 -
Baby G: Mama, what is a draft? .... - 26 -
Baby G: Mama, what is a worrywart? .... - 28 -
Baby G: Mama, what is a tattletale? .... - 30 -
Baby G: Mama, after we "go", where does it go? .... - 32 -
Baby G: Mama, how do you find out how old something is? .... - 34 -
Baby G: Mama, what is an exception? .... - 37 -
Baby G: Mama, why don't some people celebrate their birthdays? .... - 39 -
Baby G: Mama, what are skin and bones? .... - 41 -
Baby G: Mama, what are haters? .... - 43 -
Baby G: Mama, what does "too much of a good thing" mean? ..... - 48 -
Baby G: Mama, what is a deduction? .... - 50 -
Baby G: Mama, what makes things move? .... - 52 -
Baby G: Mama, what are captions? .... - 55 -
Baby G: Mama, do all animals have fur? .... - 57 -
Baby G: Mama, what does "leave the past behind" mean? .... - 59 -
Baby G: Mama, can I call someone who is in heaven? .... - 60 -
Baby G: Mama, what does "once in a blue moon" mean? .... - 62 -
Baby G: Mama, what does "practice makes perfect" mean? .... - 65 -
Baby G: Mama, what does it mean to be "afraid of one's own shadow"? .... - 67 -
Baby G: Mama, what is an average? .... - 70 -

Baby G: Mama, what does it mean to set a record? .... - 72 -
Baby G: Mama, why do camels have humps? .... - 74 -
Baby G: Mama, what is anticipation? .... - 77 -
Baby G: Mama, what are the Olympics? .... - 78 -
Baby G: Mama, what are cents? .... - 81 -
Baby G: Mama, what are special anniversaries? .... - 82 -
Baby G: Mama, what is a labor of love? .... - 85 -
Baby G: Mama, what are special birthdays? .... - 88 -
Baby G: Mama, what is a moment of silence? .... - 90 -
Baby G: Mama, what is the difference between a president and a President? .... - 92 -
Baby G: Mama, can we have our own Olympics? .... - 94 -
Baby G: Mama, what are alternatives? .... - 96 -
Baby G: Mama, what is a spectator? .... - 99 -
Baby G: Mama, what is cheating? .... - 101 -
Baby G: Mama, what does "monkey see, monkey do" mean? .... - 103 -
Baby G: Mama, what is a rumor? .... - 105 -
Baby G: Mama, what is misery? .... - 107 -
Baby G: Mama, what does "in like a lion, out like a lamb" mean? .... - 108 -
Baby G: Mama, what is World Wildlife Day? .... - 111 -
Baby G: Mama, what is the difference between seeing and observing? .... - 112 -
Baby G: Mama, what is a blindside? .... - 114 -
Baby G: Mama, what is rudeness? .... - 116 -
Baby G: Mama, what is Women's Day? .... - 118 -
Baby G: Mama, what does benign mean? .... - 120 -
Baby G: Mama, what is Daylight Savings Time? .... - 123 -
Baby G: Mama, what is a catnap? .... - 125 -
Baby G: Mama, why do you do art? .... - 126 -
Baby G: Mama, what is Pi? .... - 128 -
Baby G: Mama, what is a baby boom? .... - 130 -
Baby G: Mama, what is blarney? .... - 133 -
Baby G: Mama, what is a fake apology? .... - 135 -

v

Baby G: Mama, is it spring yet? .... - 136 -
Baby G: Mama, what does "Rock Your Socks" mean? .... - 137 -
Baby G: Mama, what is a stream? .... - 139 -
Baby G: Mama, what is patience? .... - 140 -
Baby G: Mama, what do colors mean? .... - 142 -
Baby G: Mama, what is a mishmash? .... - 144 -
Baby G: Mama, what are bears? .... - 146 -
Baby G: Mama, what is a children's song? .... - 149 -
Baby G: Mama, what does 'over' mean? .... - 152 -
Baby G: Mama, is it foolish to believe something? .... - 154 -
Baby G: Mama, why do things change? .... - 156 -
Baby G: Mama, does everyone see things the same way? .... - 158 -
Baby G: Mama, why does a rainbow have seven colors, and not just one? .... - 161 -
Baby G: Mama, what is time travel? .... - 163 -
Baby G: Mama, what does "for better, for worse" mean? .... - 165 -
Baby G: Mama, what does unique mean? .... - 167 -
Baby G: Mama, what is abuse? .... - 170 -
Baby G: Mama, what is a comfort animal? .... - 173 -
Baby G: Mama, what are the rights to life, liberty and the pursuit of happiness? ..- 176 -
Baby G: Mama, is the party all over? .... - 178 -
Baby G: Mama, what is procrastination? .... - 180 -
Baby G: Mama, what are animal crackers? .... - 182 -
Baby G: Mama, what is a cycle? .... - 185 -
Baby G: Mama, does God make mistakes? .... - 188 -
Baby G: Mama, if we didn't live on Earth, where would we live? .... - 190 -
Baby G: Mama, what does it mean to paint a picture with words? ..... - 192 -
Baby G: Mama, what is a school bus? .... - 194 -
Baby G: Mama, what does it mean to color outside the lines? .... - 197 -
Baby G: Mama, what is the home stretch? .... - 200 -
Baby G: Mama, what does it mean to come out of your shell? .... - 202 -
Baby G: Mama, what does "it is not my fault" mean? .... - 204 -

Baby G: Mama, what is May Day? .... - 207 -
Baby G: Mama, what does "don't be such a baby" mean? .... - 210 -
Baby G: Mama, what is wordplay? .... - 212 -
Baby G: Mama, what does "for the birds" mean? .... - 214 -
Baby G: Mama, what is Cinco De Mayo? .... - 216 -
Baby G: Mama, what is a Penny Dreadful? .... - 218 -
Baby G: Mama, what does it mean to reach the end of the road? .... - 220 -

Baby G: Mama, what is magic?

Summer: Baby G, if people don't know how something happened, or why it happened, if they cannot explain what caused it, they may think it happened by magic.

Willie: My jokes appear by magic. I open my mouth, and they come out. 😂

Summer: Willie, that isn't magic. Someone I know wrote your jokes for you. Just because you don't know or remember where they came from, doesn't mean someone else doesn't. Baby, some people think you can make magic by twitching your nose, blinking your eyes, waving your hand, or tapping your wand, and something will appear, or disappear, or move. If you could have special abilities, or powers, abilities most people don't have, you could perform magic. You could change or control your world with your mind.

Baby G: What would people use magic for?

Summer: You could control the weather.

Baby G: Could I make the snow and cold go away, so we could be outside more?

Summer: Yes, you could, but you would need to figure out, consider, the consequences of doing that, before you did it. When you do something, whether you do it naturally, or use magic, it may cause something else to happen. That is the consequence of what you did. It might not be a good thing.

Willie: Son, you are the consequence of what your mama and I did. That might not be a good thing. 😂

Summer: Willie! He is a great consequence! And if you weren't such a bull giraffe, you would admit you think that he is great, too. Baby, normally, in the spring, snow melts, and provides water to plants and animals. If you could magically make the snow go away now, next spring it won't be there, it won't melt, and it won't provide water. That is a bad thing. But magic is so much more than having and using special abilities. It is also a wonderful feeling, where you believe anything can happen. You feel like the world is shiny and bright, and there is always something more to see around the corner. When someone does something for someone else, just to make them happy, there is magic there.

Willie: Son, I will magically "disappear" if you close your eyes, and I shut my mouth. Then your mama can give you your lesson. That will make her happy. When Mama's not happy, nobody is happy. 😂

Summer: Thanks, Willie. You won't have to stay quiet long. Besides, your fans love it when you open your mouth, and jokes come out! Baby, when it is cold out, and we are warm in our barn, I look through my window. I see new fallen snow, icicles hanging off the trees, and a winter wonderland that is magical. The world has watched you grow from a tiny little thing to the tall, healthy, loving, and curious giraffe you are. It has been a magical journey so far. Happy eight-month birthday, Baby G.

Baby G: World, let's keep going on our journey. It will be fun, we will learn a lot, and it will be magical!

Baby G.

Tasha Poochette

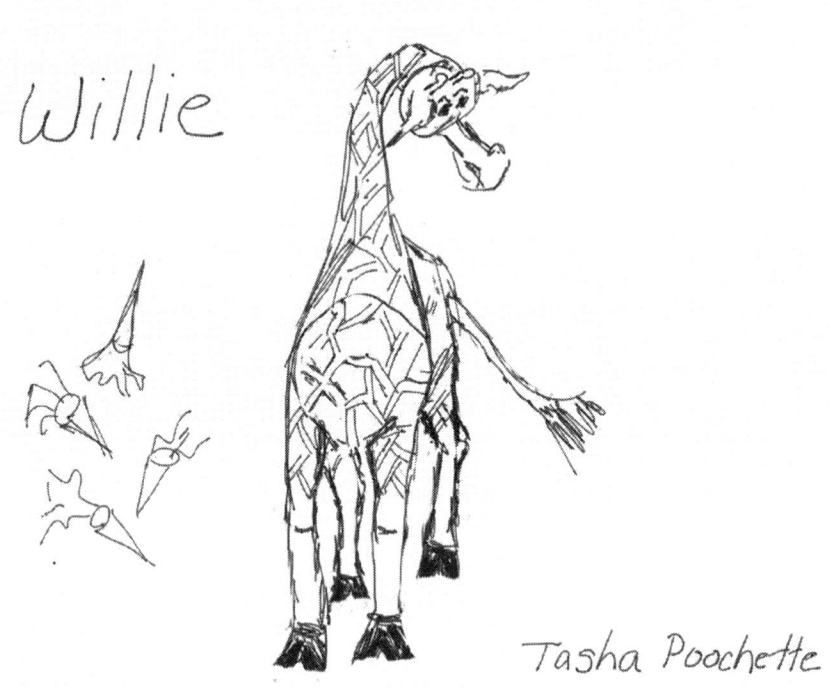

Summer

Tasha Poochette

Baby G: Mama, what is a community?

Summer: Baby G, a community is a group of people living near each other, or belonging to the same religion, or having the same race, nationality, culture, etc.

Willie: I live in the giraffe comedian community. It is a very exclusive community of one. It has gates to keep people out. I don't like being touched by my fans. 😂

Summer: Willie, if you keep to yourself, you will be lonely. You will also miss out on carrots from your fans. Baby, when people enjoy each other's company, because they share the same goals and interests, they feel like a community. Let me tell you a true story that illustrates what a community is. The people who watch us on the live cam, and chat about us, are a community. Remember, they recently pretended to be in jail, and needed 'bail' to get out, in order to raise real money for our park.

Willie: Yes, they should do it again. This time they should raise real carrots instead of real money. You can't eat money. 😂

Summer: Willie! That quote, "you cannot eat money", means if you poison or harm the source of your food, the oceans, rivers, or land, you will starve, no matter how much money you have. The real money the community raised goes to our park, and some of that goes towards buying food to feed us. Baby, they decided to do it again. The live cam watchers and chatters come from all over the world, and have different religions, races, etc. Why are they a community? They share common interests, watching and talking about us. But they don't stop there. They talk about lots of other things too, especially when the live cam is turned off. Some chatters have no one to talk to in real life, and others in the community talk to them. Some chatters need friends, and the community welcomes them. Some have very little money, or don't want to donate. The community didn't ask them to donate money. Instead, it asked them to show up, and cheer on those who did donate during the fundraiser. The community inspired people to participate in a wonderful gathering, a day long party, full of laughter and joy, that had a fantastic result. A lot of money was raised for our park. This time, the 'Jail Bail' fundraiser raised over 18,000 dollars! Everyone in the community has a common goal, to keep our park and the live cam going, so we can continue to educate the world about the plight of giraffes in the wild.

Willie: Educate them about my plight. I need a lot of money, so I can reach my goals, buying a huge carrot stash, and building a new barn to hold it. 😂

Summer: Willie, if there is a new barn, it will hold our son, and his future mate, not your carrot stash!

Baby G: World, welcome to the live cam watchers and chatters community. We enjoy your company. Together, we can do fantastic things like help the giraffes in the wild.

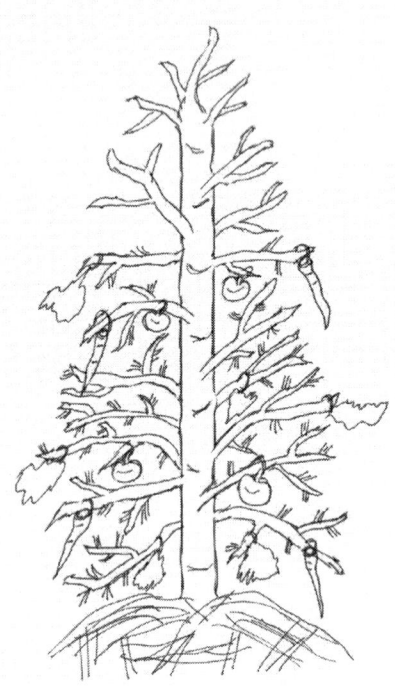

Willie's Tree

Tasha Poochette

Baby G: Mama, what are traditions?
Summer: Baby G, a tradition is something you do every year. Traditions are also beliefs, customs, information, or behaviors passed from generation to generation.
Willie: Son, you are a family addition. It is my belief that it is customary to pass information about bull giraffe behavior to the next generation, you. It is a train-addition. 😂
Summer: Willie, that word is tradition, not 'train-addition'. But you are right, we should both train our son, and pass family traditions to him. Baby, some people decorate Christmas trees, some go to midnight mass (at a church) or go to sunrise services, and many sing Christmas carols. Other people light one candle in a Hanukkah menorah each night for eight nights, some say prayers, and many eat special foods like latkes (potato pancakes).
Willie: I have my own traditions. I joke about food, sing "Food, glorious food…", pray for more food, and eat special foods like carrotkes (carrot pancakes). 😂
Summer: Willie! Pray we don't throw rotten tomatoes at you. Let us talk. Baby, a lot of people exchange gifts during one of these holidays, or even during both holidays. Today is the Winter Solstice, the shortest day of the year. It is also the longest night of the year. Some people call it Yule. Some eat special foods like Yule logs, nuts, pomegranates and watermelons. All of these activities are holiday traditions.
Baby: Does everyone have the same traditions everywhere?
Summer: No, they don't. Even the ones that share the same traditions may not celebrate in exactly the same way. Some may put gifts in stockings, some under the tree, and some in a shoe. Some visit Santa, others welcome Father

Christmas or St. Nick. Each country, and each family, has its own traditions.

Baby G: Do traditions ever change?

Summer: Yes. Over the years, all over the world, people have changed their traditions, or started new ones. Families change: babies are born; children grow up; some family members move away; and some are lost. New people may join the family. Family traditions may change too. After you grow up, you can decide whether, and how, you want to celebrate anything. You can continue your family's traditions or start your own traditions. Some families celebrate a baby's first Christmas, by putting a special ornament on the tree, and putting new ornaments on every year. When the children grow up, and move to their own homes, they take their ornaments, to put on their own trees.

Willie: My tree is decorated with carrots, and lettuce, and apples. Instead of a tree skirt that resembles snow, it has alfalfa hay from your mama's hay showers. She likes to redecorate our barn. The top of the tree is bare. I got hungry. 😂

Baby G: World, I would love to know about your family's traditions. How do you celebrate?

Baby G: Mama, what are Christmas carols?

Willie: A bunch of lady giraffes named Carol got together to sing. They called themselves the Christmas Carols. But it was confusing when the conductor tried to tell a Carol to carol some carols in front of the other Carols. 😂

Summer: Willie, Christmas carols are songs, not lady giraffes named Carol! Baby G, some Christmas carols tell the Christmas story, some spread good cheer, and some are about Santa.

Baby G: Which ones tell the Christmas story?

Summer: Some inspirational Christmas songs tell about The First Noel, which was on a Silent Night, when the Christ child was born, Away in a Manger, in O Little Town of Bethlehem, bringing Joy to the World. Do You Hear What I Hear? Angels We Have Heard on High. Hark! The Herald Angels Sing about the birth, and say, O Come, All Ye Faithful, to adore him. Many, like We Three Kings, come bearing gifts or give services instead of gifts, like the Little Drummer Boy.

Baby G: Which ones spread good cheer?

Summer: I'll Be Home for Christmas. Baby It's Cold Outside, Let It Snow Let It Snow Let It Snow, we want a White Christmas, where there are Silver Bells, Jingle Bells, and a Sleigh Ride. We Wish You a Merry Christmas. Deck The Halls, and decorate O Christmas Tree, while we visit with Frosty the Snowman. It's the Most Wonderful Time of the Year. Have Yourself A Merry Little Christmas, but remember to help those in need, like Good King Wenceslas did.

Willie: I am Giraffe King Willie. I help those in need, like me. I need my fans, my royal subjects, to bring me more carrots! 😂

Summer: Willie! You aren't a king, you have no royal subjects, and besides, at Christmas, you should help others, and not yourself.

Baby G: Which ones are about Santa?

Summer: Santa Claus Is Comin' To Town. Here Comes Santa Claus, Up on the Housetop. I Saw Mommy Kissing Santa Claus, Jolly Old St. Nicholas. Oh no, Grandma Got Run Over by a Reindeer. Don't worry, it wasn't Rudolph, the Red-Nosed Reindeer.

Baby G: Does everyone enjoy Christmas carols?

Summer: Many people do. Some people don't celebrate Christmas, so they don't like inspirational Christmas carols. But they might enjoy the cheerful songs about happy holidays, snow, bells, etc.

Willie: I enjoy the songs about happy holidays, but not the ones about snow. Giraffes don't do well in snow. They may fall and get their bells rung. 😂

Summer: Willie, most of the holiday songs are about staying inside, where it is warm, not about being IN the snow. Baby, some people normally do celebrate Christmas, but now they are alone, they have no family or friends, or they are sick, or they have little money for Christmas gifts. They might not feel joyful at Christmas time.

Baby G: World, Merry Christmas, if you celebrate Christmas, and Happy Holidays, if you don't. If you do, enjoy your Christmas, spread some cheer, and sing some carols, but don't forget those who don't have what you have.

Willie's
   Carrot
      Servants

Tasha Poochette

Baby G: Mama, what are servants?

Summer: Baby G, servants are people who work for others. They serve them food, help them dress, clean their homes, etc.

Willie: We have carrot servants that are falling down on the job, we didn't get any carrots today. We should fire them. 😂

Summer: Willie, giraffes don't have servants! When our fans refer to themselves as our "carrot servants", it is a joke. They give us carrots because they want to, not because they must. Baby, typically, a servant is paid money for the work they do. In exchange for money, they take orders from their employers. They are told what to do, and when to do it. They are expected to do it. If they don't, they are fired. They lose their jobs.

Willie: I like being able to order people around. The problem is humans can't hear giraffes hum, so they can't hear my orders. 😂

Summer: Willie! You don't get to order humans around! Our human family volunteers to take care of us, because, like our fans, they want to make us happy, and keep us healthy. Some people are paid to take care of us, but they answer to their boss, their employer, and not to us.

Baby G: Do servants like being servants?

Summer: Some do, and some don't. Some enjoy the work they do. Some take pride in doing a good job of taking care of their employers. Others are just doing the work for the money, or they hate their employers, and can't wait to get a different job. Servants are just one type of employee. Many people don't like taking orders. But so long as you work for someone else, if you are a paid employee, you must take orders. So, for many, their dream is to work for themselves.

Employers need to remember that employees are not slaves, and to treat their employees well. They need to thank them for their services. There is another kind of servant who is not paid, they volunteer to serve others. They do not take orders from humans, but from God.

Baby G: Is today a holiday?

Summer: Not here. But in some places, the day after Christmas is Boxing Day.

Willie: Yeah, Boxing Day is when you get into a boxing ring with those people who didn't give you what you wanted for Christmas, and you try to punch them in the nose. 😂

Summer: Willie, gifts are gifts! No one is forced to give you anything. You thank the giver, even if you are disappointed. You don't punch anyone in the nose! Baby, in the past, servants in those places were thanked for their service. They were given boxes with money, food, cloth, or gifts. Today, Boxing Day is a day to recover from Christmas, spend time with family and friends, do or watch sports, or go shopping.

Baby G: World, no matter whether you are the kind of servant, or employee, who does it for the money, or who takes pride in a job well done, or who serves others for God, thanks for your service.

Baby G: Mama, what does "follow your heart" mean?
Willie: It means follow your mama's heart patterns, and her, around and around. Shouldn't that expression be "follow her hearts"? 😂
Summer: Willie, "follow your heart" doesn't mean you should follow my heart patterns! Baby G, that expression, "follow your heart", means you should do what you really love to do, or what you believe is the right thing to do. Focus on, pay attention to, what truly matters to you. Listen to your heart and do what you believe will make you happy.
Baby G: My heart talks?
Summer: Not really. That expression, "listen to your heart", means stop thinking so much about things, and pay attention to your emotions, your feelings, what you really want.
Baby G: How will I know what makes me happy, and what truly matters to me?
Willie: I really love to follow your mama. As soon as our human family opens the gate between our pens, I closely follow her. It makes me happy. It is the right thing to do, and it truly matters to me, because I am a bull giraffe. You are a bull giraffe too. Pay attention to what we do and learn. She hums, "Follow me when I go, smell what I do, your nose will know...". 😂
Summer: Willie! He is still too young to learn that! Baby, pay no attention to Daddy!
Baby G: I shouldn't pay attention, and learn from Daddy?
Summer: Yes, you should, but you don't need this lesson now.
Baby G: Why do I have to wait? I want to know everything now!
Summer: You will be three years old before you need to know about that. Be patient. You'll grow up soon enough. Humans must wait much longer than giraffes to grow up. Anyway, that song really goes like this: "Follow me where I go, what I do, and who I know...". It means be with me, share my life, and join me on my journey. As you grow, you will learn about, and try many new things. You will discover what you like, what you don't, what you love, and what you hate.

Willie: I hate fish and beets. I tell them to beat it and leave my plate. 😂
Summer: Willie, giraffes don't eat fish, and you have never eaten beets! Baby, if you give a new food a fair chance, and try it, and you still hate it, you shouldn't be forced to eat it. But you can't reject new foods without trying them once and expect to be given other food instead. Your home is not a restaurant. But I am not just talking about food now. On your journey, you will find out what truly matters to you, what is important to you, and what you love to do. You will learn what is the right thing to do in many new situations.
Baby G: World, follow your heart, and do what you believe is the right thing to do. Focus on what truly matters to you. Do what you really love to do. I love sharing my journey with you.

Baby G: Mama, what is a snow day?

Willie: I am waiting for your mama to tell me when it's nose day. I use my nose, and ... 😂

Summer: Willie, he asked about a snow day, not a nose day! Baby G, when there is a lot of snow, human kids can stay home from school, and play. It is a snow day.

Baby G: Do adults get to stay home too?

Summer: If the snow is coming down very hard, and fast, or a lot of snow is blowing around, that is a blizzard, a severe snowstorm, with strong winds. Most adults stay home during blizzards. When you can only see white snowflakes in the air, and white snow on the ground, when you can't see the road, signs, trees, or buildings alongside the road, it is called a whiteout. It is very dangerous to drive in whiteout conditions. You have no idea where the edges of the road are.

Baby G: Is snow always dangerous?

Summer: Yes, snow is always dangerous for us giraffes. We can never go outside when there is snow, or it is too cold. It is not always dangerous for humans, but they still need to be careful, to not slip and fall on ice, and to stay warm. Humans can go outside if the snow stops falling hard or blowing around. They must wear warm clothes, hats on their heads, gloves or mittens on their hands, and boots on their feet.

Baby G: What do humans do in the snow?

Summer: They throw snowballs at each other, build snowmen, make snow angels, go skiing, go snowboarding, go sledding, etc. Skis, snowboards, and sleds slide on snow. Humans wear special shoes, ice skates, to safely slip or skate on ice.

Willie: I try to tell your mama to slip into something more comfortable. She tells me I am skating on thin ice. 😂

Baby G: Do any animals live in the snow?

Summer: Polar bears, Arctic foxes, Arctic wolves, and other animals live in the snow. They have thick fur to keep them warm. Penguins are flightless birds. They cannot fly. Some penguins live on ice.

Baby G: Where do those animals live?

Summer: At the top of the world is the North Pole. At the bottom is the South Pole. Around the poles, there are the Arctic and Antarctic regions. They are very cold and have a lot of snow and ice. The polar bears, Arctic foxes and Arctic wolves live in the Arctic region. Some penguins live in the Antarctic region.

Baby G: Does every place get snow?

Summer: No. It must be cold enough, and there must be enough moisture, water, in the air for snow to form. The best of all worlds is to live where it doesn't snow but be able to travel to places where it does snow, when you want to play in it.

Willie: When I interrupt your lessons, your mama gives me the cold shoulder. It is really cold. Brrr. 😂

Summer: Willie, the best of all worlds is to learn when it is time to let him learn, and when it is your time. You will get a warmer reception from me.

Baby G: World, when there is snow, or it is too cold, keep us captive giraffes inside, where it is safe and warm. Don't let us go outside, where it is dangerous for us. Enjoy playing in the snow, if you live in areas that get snow, or can travel there. I hope it doesn't snow too hard, or too fast. Be safe and stay warm.

Baby G: Mama, what does "better late than never" mean?
Summer: Baby G, that expression, "better late than never", means if you start to do something late, it is better than never doing it at all. Of course, doing it on time is better still.
Willie: Someone said, "Call me anything you like, just don't call me late for dinner". I say calling me late to dinner is better than never. 😂
Summer: Willie, go find something to eat, and let us talk. Baby, the lady who writes about our conversations wanted to write about the ones on New Year's Eve, and New Year's Day, but she was busy. But it is better late than never, so she will write about them now.
Baby G: What did we talk about?
Summer: You asked what all the noises were. I said people were banging pots and pans, tooting horns, shooting fireworks, and cheering the end of the old year, 2017, and the beginning of the new year, 2018. They were remembering the year that ended, and what happened, and celebrating the new year, and a fresh start. Last year, with all of the hurricanes, earthquakes, wildfires, and other natural disasters, and so much bad news, was a hard year for many people. They are hoping 2018 will be better.
Baby G: Right, and I asked you what the best parts of 2017 for you were, Mama.
Summer: I said your birth, teaching you, and watching you grow.
Baby G: You asked me what my favorite parts were, and I said learning, and having the world join me on my journey.
Willie: I said the best parts were when our human family let us all be together without a fence between us, and I could

be fresh with your mama. I am all for starting fresh and staying that way! 😂

Summer: Willie! Admit it, our baby was, and is, the highlight of our year, and our life together! Baby, we also talked about New Year's resolutions. When you make a resolution, you resolve to change something bad about yourself, or to stop doing something bad, or to do something new, or to keep doing something good.

Baby G: I resolved to keep learning about my family, giraffes, other animals, humans, and the world.

Summer: I resolved to keep educating you about the plight of giraffes in the wild, so you can continue to share what you learn with the world. I also resolved to lose the last of my baby weight, weight I gained while making you.

Willie: I resolved to cast off the old baby, you, and make your mama gain new baby weight, with a new baby! 😂

Summer: Willie, the old baby isn't him, and it isn't a baby! It is a very old man, Father Time. Baby, in pictures, Father Time symbolizes, represents, the old year, and a new baby symbolizes the new year. We are giraffes, and making a baby takes fifteen months for us. If we make a new baby, it will not show up until 2019. It will be a long time before I gain any visible weight, unless it is from food, and not a baby!

Baby G: World, whether last year was good or bad for you, I hope the new year will be even better for you. If you have already broken, or failed to make, your New Year's resolutions, you can start again. Better late than never!

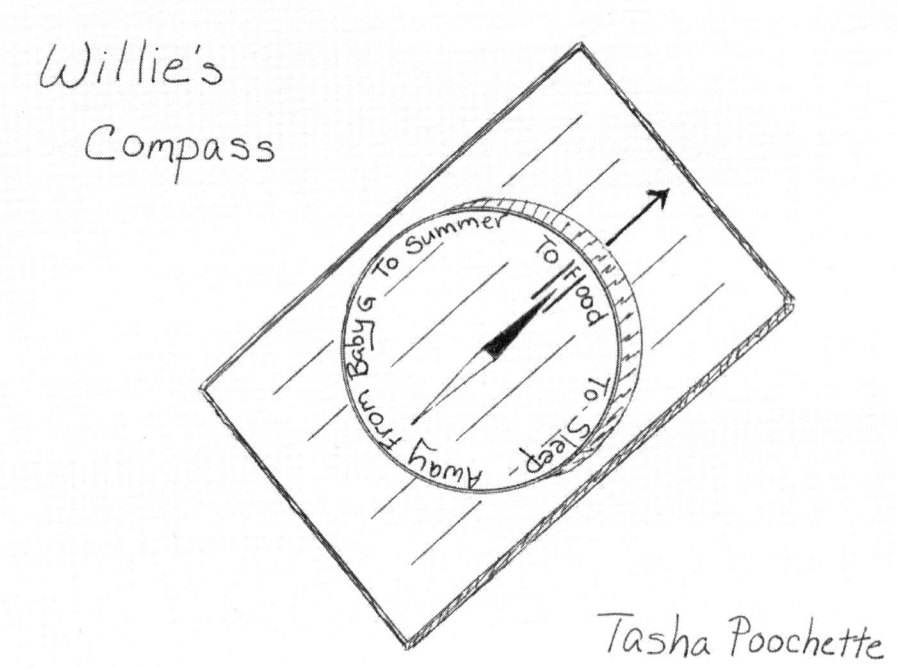

Willie's Compass

Tasha Poochette

Baby G: Mama, what are directions?

Summer: Baby G, directions are instructions on how to do something, or how to go from one place to another place.

Willie: There is an old joke, why were Moses and the Israelites lost in the desert for forty years? Even then, men could not follow directions. 😂

Summer: Willie, please follow my direction, leave us, and let us talk. Baby, your direction is the path on which you are moving, or the position you are facing. North, East, South, and West are directions, points on a compass.

Baby G: What is a compass?

Summer: A compass is something with a dial and a rotating needle on it. The red end of the needle always points to magnetic North. You can use the compass to figure out what direction you are facing. If the needle points straight ahead of you, then you are facing North. If the needle points towards you, that means your back is towards the North, and you are facing the opposite direction, South. A compass, like a circle, has 360 degrees.

Willie: My compass has four directions: go towards food, go to sleep, go away from you, and go towards Summer. 😂

Summer: Willie! Your compass needs a fifth one: go in the opposite direction! Baby, a compass is used with a map to figure out how to get somewhere. Maps usually point North on top. You hold the compass, turn yourself around, and move the compass dial, until the N (for North) mark, the orienting lines or arrow, and the direction of travel arrow on the compass are all lined up with the red end of the needle. Then you will be facing North. What if you want to go in a different direction, like West? You place the compass on the map and rotate the compass in order to point the direction of travel arrow in the direction you want

to go, West. Move the dial so the N mark, and the orienting lines or arrow, are lined up with the red end of the needle again. Pick up the compass and hold it so that the direction of travel arrow points straight ahead of you. If you turn yourself until the red end of the compass needle is back inside the orienting lines, pointing to the N mark, and you keep the direction of travel arrow pointing straight ahead of you, you will be going in the right direction, and will get to where you want to go. Some phones have compass apps that automatically move the compass dial for you. Some have map apps. Some have a GPS system that tells you where you are, and how to get to where you want to go. But GPS systems, map apps, and cell phones don't work everywhere. It is still good to know how to use a compass.
Baby G: What if you don't have any of them?
Summer: Long ago, people navigated by the stars. The Big Dipper constellation looks like a cup with a curved handle. Look at the two outermost stars in the cup (on the side of the cup opposite the handle). See the distance between those two stars. Move your eyes along the side of the cup for five times that distance, and you will find the bright North Star, Polaris. The Southern Cross can also be used to navigate.
Baby G: What if it is daytime, and you cannot see the stars?
Willie: Just bump your head, and you will see plenty of stars. 😂
Summer: In the northern hemisphere, more moss grows on the north side of trees.
Baby G: World, I hope you are never lost, and always know how to get where you want to go. Use directions, a map and a compass, or a GPS system, to help you get there.

Baby G: Mama, what is a spectacle?
Summer: Baby G, a spectacle is a visually striking show or display. It is something worth watching. You look at it, and say, "Wow". A spectacle can also be a bad thing, where someone makes a fool out of themselves. You look at them in contempt, with disdain, or with scorn. You despise them, or you despise what they are doing. You say that person made a spectacle of themselves. Spectacles are another name for eyeglasses.

Willie: Did you ever see such a spectacle as a giraffe in spectacles?
Baby G: Why is that a spectacle?
Summer: Giraffes have phenomenal eyesight, and don't need to wear eyeglasses.
Willie: I want to use my phenomenal eyesight to see something phenomenal far away, all the lady giraffes putting on a show at Cheyenne Mountain Zoo.
Summer: Willie! You will have a phenomenal black eye after I get done with you! Stop eyeing those lady giraffes!
Baby G: What are eyeglasses?
Summer: Humans sometimes need eyeglasses, also called glasses, to see far away. Some need glasses to see anything. Older humans often need glasses to read things that are near them.
Baby G: So, glasses are a good thing?
Summer: Yes, they are. But sometimes children feel bad about having to wear glasses because other children may tease them. Some kids can't see well, some cannot hear well, some have problems moving, and some have messed up faces or bodies. Children can be not nice to kids who are different than them. They can be mean.
Baby G: Won't those mean children need glasses, or some other help, themselves someday?
Summer: They probably will, and then they may feel sorry for ever teasing anyone. But children often just think about right now, and not someday.
Willie: I am not nice to our son because he is NOT different from me. We are both bull giraffes, and normally bull giraffes don't hang out together. We fight. Maybe we could hang out together to watch the fights?
Summer: Willie, you are right, bull giraffes don't hang out together in the wild, but that is not true here in captivity. Be the adult you are and be nice to your son. Accept him. Spend time together. You will discover he is fun to be with.
Baby G: World, be nice to people who are different than you. They are more like you than you think. Everyone wants to be liked, to be accepted, to have someone to spend time with, and someone to have fun with!

Baby G: Mama, what is a draft?

Summer: Baby G, a rough draft is a first attempt to write something. You redo it several times, creating more preliminary drafts, until it is finally the way you want it. A draft is also a way to get new members for a football team, or to recruit new people into military service. They are drafted.

Willie: A draft giraffe is a special type of giraffe that drinks longneck beers and is built like a tank. He is really heavy. 😂

Summer: Willie, you are mixing up draft beer, which comes from a tank or a barrel, not a longneck bottle, with a draft animal, like a horse or an ox, that pulls heavy loads. Baby, a draft, which is also called a draught in some places, can be cold air coming under a door, or through holes in the wall. Our human family puts a draft blocker, made of hay, by the bottom of our door, to block the cold air from entering our barn.

Baby G: I thought that was our midnight snack bar?

Summer: No. They use something we can eat to ensure we don't get sick nibbling on something we cannot eat.

Baby G: What can't we eat?

Summer: We can't eat anything that is toxic, anything that would make us sick. We can't eat plastic, paint, lead, and many more things. We can only eat food: leaves, hay, grain, carrots, apples, etc. Human babies need to be kept away from toxic things, because they put everything in their mouths. They need to grow up a little and learn what not to eat.

Baby G: Can humans eat more food than we can?

Willie: No, they can't. We weigh up to 2800 lbs., and humans are much lighter. There is not enough room in them to eat as much food as we eat. Although some of them try. 😂

Summer: Willie! They can eat more TYPES of food, including chocolate, than giraffes can. Dogs cannot eat chocolate. It contains theobromine, which is toxic to dogs. Keep all chocolate away from dogs.

Baby G: If we eat our draft blocker, and the cold air gets into our barn, where does it go?

Summer: Our barn has heaters to heat up the air. Because of something called convection, warm air rises, cools off, and sinks again. The air moves in a circle. It is warmer up by our heads than by our feet. It is very warm up in the loft. So, if there are holes in our ceiling or roof, or holes high up in our walls, the warm, heated, air escapes out the holes. The cold air keeps coming in under our door, to replace the lost warm air. The cold air comes in faster than the heaters can warm it, making us cold. Our human family is fixing the holes near the ceiling, so the warm air will stay in our barn, and not be lost.

Baby G: Are there other ways of heating stuff up?

Summer: Yes. When sunlight hits the dark ground, the visible (light) radiation is turned into infrared (heat) radiation that warms the air. Conventional ovens and microwaves use radiation to cook food.

Willie: Summer, let us cuddle. I will conduct myself like a gentle giraffe, and let conduction warm you up. 😂

Summer: Willie, that expression is "conduct yourself like a gentleman", not a gentle giraffe. Baby, when two things touch, and one is warmer than the other, and the first one passes heat to the other, that is called conduction. When you are cold, cuddling, and sharing body heat, is a good thing.

Baby G: World, it is really cold outside. Stay warm, and fix anything that allows warm air to escape. The warm air is good for you, unlike toxic things. Stay away from them.

Baby G: Mama, what is a worrywart?

Summer: Baby G, a worrywart is someone who often worries about things. Usually, they worry about things they don't need to worry about. They are fearful or apprehensive. They constantly think something bad will happen. Sometimes, they don't understand how something works, or how unimportant, how trivial, something is. Other times, they don't understand that someone else knows what happened, and what to do. The worrywart may not trust someone else to do the right thing.

Willie: They make a big ado about nothing. Or they make a play called Much Ado About Nothing. Or they make a whole TV series about nothing. 😂

Summer: Willie, to the worrywart, it isn't nothing. Baby, it is true, they often make a big fuss over a minor event. They keep talking about it and stressing over it. They may send emails to someone about it. They report what they see, or what they think they saw.

Willie: Yeah, I was startled. I moved too fast, I stumbled, and fell to my knees. I am fine, but some worrywart, watching the live cam, stumbled over themselves to fire off an email about my stumble. Gee, you gotta give a guy a chance to save face, and pretend his stumble was deliberate! Maybe I was kneeling in prayer, that they would forget I was still in your pen, when your mama and you returned to it? 😂

Summer: Willie, giraffes can't kneel in prayer! But you are right, that worrywart should not have sent that email.

Baby G: Aren't emails a good thing?

Summer: Yes, usually they are. But when you send a lot of unwanted emails to someone, they are called spam emails. When someone sends an email to our human family, telling them how to take care of us, that is insulting to them. They know how to take care of us, and they do it very well. Look at how healthy we are. Our human family, and their employees, need to spend their time caring for us, and the other animals in our park, not reading or answering unwanted emails.

Baby G: Aren't the live cam watchers helping by reporting what they see?

Summer: They think they are, but our human family watches us in person, and watches the cam too. They usually know what is going on with us. They know we aren't eating toxic materials when we lick or chew on our doors. They know that because they don't use, or leave, toxic stuff in our pens. Every stumble we make doesn't require a doctor to visit. If something really is wrong, they will fix it, or get our doctor to help. Also, given the location and angle of the cam, large things can look small, and small details may be missed. The cam watchers may not see what really happens or know the details about how our barn was made, what is on the floor, or on the doors, or in the roof. It is best to not send emails about what you see on the live cam.

Willie: Watchers, send them emails demanding more carrots for me. As you can plainly see, I am starving to death. I didn't just stumble, I almost fell over from lack of food, tell them! 😂

Summer: Willie! You clearly are overweight and are not starving to death! Baby, emails like that are not correct, not wanted, and not needed. Trust our human family to do the right thing.

Baby G: World, I love that you watch us, care about us, and follow my journey. Trust that our human family also watches, cares about us, and knows what to do.

Baby G: Mama, what is a tattletale?

Willie: I follow your mama very closely every chance I get. I can say, with authority, that she doesn't have a tattoo on her tail. There is no tat-on-tail. 😂

Summer: Willie, he asked about a tattletale, not a tat-on-tail! Baby G, a tattletale is someone who tattles about what you are doing. They tell someone in authority, like a parent or teacher, what you did. If you are doing something illegal, or you will hurt yourself, or you are planning to hurt others, then it is good for someone to tell what you are doing. They are not a tattletale. But if someone else tattles on you, just to get you in trouble, or because they want you out of the way, so they can do something themselves, that is bad. Sometimes, a tattletale just wants attention. They think a parent or teacher will be pleased with them if they tattle. Usually, a tattletale is a child, but adults can be tattletales too. They sometimes act like children, and they tattle to another adult. Don't be a tattletale.

Willie: I would tattle that your mama wastes the hay she uses in her hay showers, but I don't know whom I could tell. We are the only adults here. 😂

Summer: Willie! I don't waste the hay I use in my hay showers! Your son and I eat that hay later. Baby, a tattletale may think they see something bad, but it may not actually be bad. Your daddy didn't realize the hay can be eaten later. So, he was upset because he thought my hay showers are wasteful, but they really aren't.

Baby G: So, people get upset, and tattle about things they shouldn't?

Summer: In the live cam chat, someone may get upset if they don't like what someone else said. The right thing to do is to ignore that person, especially if that person is a troll. Enjoy chatting with the rest of the people. Don't let one person drive you away, or make you stop chatting. But some people don't ignore trolls or topics they don't like. They wait until the owner of the chat site or group, or an administrator, or a moderator, someone with authority, gets on the live chat, and they tattle about who said what, and when they said it.

Baby G: So, you should not tell anyone who the trolls are?

Willie: I'd tell people who the trolls are, but I don't know who they are. I don't read the live chat, because I cannot read that fast. It scrolls by too fast. 😂

Summer: Willie, you can stop the chat from scrolling by clicking or tapping on it. Baby, wait until you are asked to name the trolls. Don't rush to tattle. Often, a troll will be zapped, and not allowed to chat anymore. This is not because someone tattled, but because the troll is stupid enough to act like the troll they are, while someone in authority is in the chat. They can see for themselves who is actually a troll, and who is just talking about something you may not like. You cannot control what people talk about, so long as they keep the chat friendly, they are not attacking anyone, and they don't talk about any banned topics. Only the person in authority can say what topics are banned. You can only control how you respond to what someone says. Ignore what you do not like and start new chats about what you do like.

Baby G: World, unless someone is doing something illegal, or will hurt themselves, or will hurt others, don't be a tattletale. Ignore trolls and topics you don't like. Start a new chat about what you do like. Keep the chat friendly, and don't attack anyone.

Baby G: Mama, after we "go", where does it go?
Summer: Baby G, before I tell you that, let's talk about food and drink.
Willie: Yeah, I would rather talk about food and drink, unless we are talking about your mama's ... 😂
Summer: Willie, don't waste our time, he is still too young to learn that! Baby, you eat food, and drink liquids like water, milk, etc. Your body takes what it needs, to keep you alive, help your body heal itself, help you grow, and give you energy, so you can move. Some of the extra is stored as fat. You gain weight. What remains is waste. Your body gets rid of it.
Willie: Hurry and get potty trained. You are ten feet tall, weigh a lot, eat a lot, and waste a lot. I don't like changing your diaper! 😂
Summer: Willie! Giraffes don't wear diapers! Baby, if you are an animal, you urinate (pee) or defecate (poop) almost anywhere. You shouldn't do it where you eat or sleep. If you are a human baby, you wear a diaper, or a nappy. You go when you need to go, and then your parents change your diaper or nappy. Later, you are potty trained. You tell your parents, or yourself, that you have to go to the bathroom. In some places, it is the restroom, the water closet, the outhouse, etc. You use the toilet, the latrine, the john, the loo, etc. You do "number one" (pee) or "number two" (poop). The waste enters a city sewage system, a septic tank in your yard, etc.
Baby G: So, animals are not potty trained?
Summer: Some animals, like dogs and cats, can be housebroken. The dogs wait to go until they are outside. Humans need to use a bag, pick up their dog's waste, and put it into the trash. The cats use a litter box that needs to

be changed often. Some city horses carry bags under their tails to catch the waste.

Baby G: What happens to animal waste?

Summer: Some animals, like cows and horses, produce waste, manure, that can be used as fertilizer, food for plants. The cow pies are smelly, and look icky, but they make great fertilizer if spread around. There is a quote, "Money is like manure, it's only good if you spread it around".

Baby G: Is giraffe manure good for anything?

Willie: They should charge for my manure. It is full of precious jokes. I often eat my own words. 😂

Summer: Willie, you are full of it, alright. But your manure is the same as any other giraffe's. We all eat the same food. Baby, our manure is shoveled up by our human family when they clean our pens, and sent to a farm, to be used as fertilizer for their plants. Later, the plants become food for animals in our park. It is a cycle. Eat plants, poop waste, clean pens, spread manure, fertilize other plants so they will grow, eat plants. Human manure is not used as fertilizer because of the variety of foods they eat, and the drugs they use. Touching it, or ingesting it, can make humans sick.

Baby G: World, manure may be icky, it may be smelly, but spreading around the right kind of manure does good, and helps plants grow. Make sure the other kind goes where it is supposed to go. You don't want to get sick.

Baby G: Mama, how do you find out how old something is?
Summer: Baby G, that depends. Trees have concentric growth rings or circles. Concentric circles are circles, often different sizes, that have the same center. Each year, as it grows, the tree gets another ring. You can cut across the tree trunk and count the rings.
Willie: I cut across to your mama, she moves toward you, you try to get out of her way, and follow me. Round and round we go. People think we are playing "Ring Around the Rosie". I'd rather play a different game with your mama, while you go smell the roses. 😂
Summer: Willie, stop playing games now, and let us talk. Baby, you can roughly tell how old a horse is by its teeth. An aged horse or person is "long in the tooth". Old horses have teeth that are long, sharply angled, and have special grooves. The groove length tells you how old the horse is. If you know the birthdate or creation date for something, you subtract it from the current year, and you will know how old it is. You could ask pet owners when their pets were born. They may have birth records. They may have been present during the births. The world watched you being born and will never forget when that happened.
Baby G: Who else has records?
Summer: Works of art, antiques, and other objects may have provenance, historical records, of who owned them, and when they were created, or sold. Some animals, like horses and captive giraffes, may be listed in a registry, or a studbook. The listing says when and where they were born, who their parents and ancestors were, who their descendants are, etc.
Willie: I have a studbook showing all my descendants. The problem is I only have one descendant, you. It is a thin studbook. 😂
Summer: Willie, be patient. You are still very young and have a lifetime to have more descendants. Baby, humans usually have birth certificates, but sometimes birth certificates can't be found.
Baby G: Can I just ask people how old they are?
Summer: It is usually considered rude to ask someone's age. They might not care and may freely tell you what you want to know. They may not answer, because they don't know, or they are so old they forget how old they are, or they are too young to talk. In that case,

maybe you can ask their parents. Sometimes, there are no records, or the records cannot be found, and there is nobody to ask. You might be able to look at the design or craftsmanship of something and know roughly when or where it was made. The earth has a lot of carbon in it. Diamonds are made from carbon. Every living thing has carbon in it. After it dies, it still has carbon in it. Over a very long time, the carbon changes from one form, one isotope, to another form. By comparing how much of each form remains, you can figure out how old something is. That is called carbon dating.
Willie: I thought carbon dating was when you give someone a diamond, made of carbon, so they will keep dating you. 😂
Summer: Willie! Humans give their future mates real diamonds as a sign of their love and commitment, not so they will keep dating them! Every real diamond is almost as old as the earth, they were made under extremely high heat and pressure, and no new ones are being made.
Baby G: World, you all know how old I am. I won't ask how old you are, I don't want to be rude. But join me in finding out how old things are. It is fun to discover when they were created, who or what created them, and where they come from!

Giraffe in deep snow

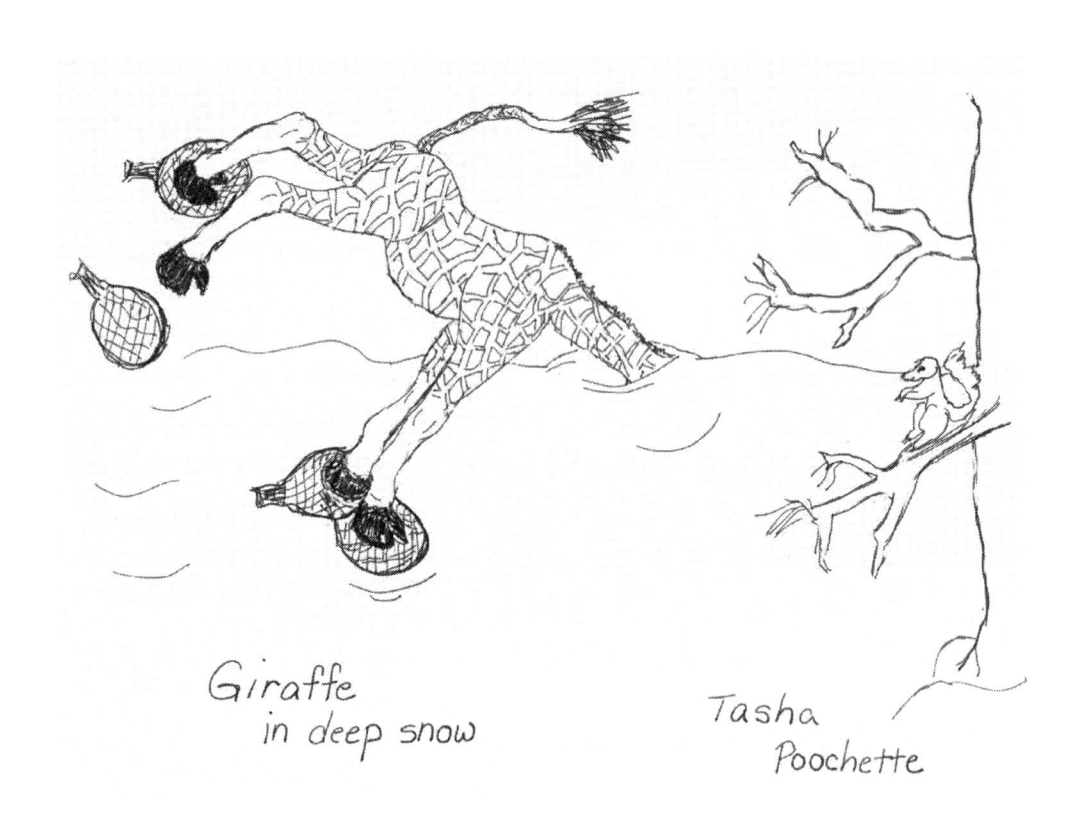

Tasha Poochette

Baby G: Mama, what is an exception?
Summer: Baby G, an exception is someone, or something, that does not follow a rule.
Willie: I make a point of never following rules, without exception. But that is a rule too, so if I follow my rule, there is an exception to never following rules. 😂
Summer: Willie, you are exceptional at choosing the wrong time to interrupt us. Baby, if something is no exception to a rule, it does follow that rule. If you make an exception, you do something different than what is usual for you, what you normally do.
Baby G: I don't understand.
Summer: For example, a rule says, 'we captive giraffes should be kept inside, when there is snow, or it is too cold'. It is a pain to follow that rule, because we don't want to stay inside all winter. However, the rule keeps us safe. We don't want to slip and fall or be cold. The exception to this rule is, if it is warm enough outside, and there is no ice, we can go out in the snow. Water freezes, and becomes ice, at 32 degrees Fahrenheit. Ice melts, and becomes liquid water again, at 33F or higher. Yesterday, it was way over that. So, there was no chance of ice, and the snow was melting. Our human family made an exception to the rule and let us go outside in the snow. How did you like it?
Baby G: It was strange. It made my feet cold. It was odd that when I stepped on it, my feet went down in it. The ground is normally brown, but the snow made it white.
Summer: That is another exception. The ground is normally brown, except after snow falls on it. Then it is white. Humans wear boots, when walking in snow, to keep their feet warm. They may use snowshoes to walk on top of snow, to prevent their boots from sinking into it. A

snowshoe has a lightweight, oval or racket shaped frame, with a network of leather or synthetic material straps stretched across it. Snowshoes spread the weight of the person over a larger area, so their boots don't sink into the snow.

Willie: Our feet are already as big as dinner plates, and I am a bull giraffe. We weigh a ton. How big would giraffe snowshoes have to be to keep my weight from sinking all of me, not just my boots, into the deep snow? 😂

Summer: Willie! Giraffes don't wear boots or snowshoes! There is no exception to the rule 'giraffes can't walk in deep snow'! Baby, new fallen, fresh, snow is pure white, but it can get dirty as it melts.

Baby G: I put my head down, but I wasn't sure if I was supposed to eat the snow.

Summer: It is generally safe to eat snow, or to melt it, so you can drink it, but there are some exceptions. As snow falls, it may collect bad stuff from the air, like dust. Once it hits the ground, it may pick up pesticides, chemicals, algae, and dirt. These things discolor the snow, changing it from pure white, to red, green, brown, or other colors. Animals sometimes pee in snow, making it yellow. So, another rule is 'only eat snow that is pure white'. It is fun to stick your tongue out and catch snowflakes.

Willie: Every snowflake is unique, not like any other. Just like every Willie is not like this Willie. I am the only giraffe comedian named Willie! 😂

Baby G: World, some rules can be a pain to follow, but they exist to keep you safe. I enjoyed the exception to the 'we captive giraffes should be kept inside, when there is snow, or it is too cold.' rule. But there are no exceptions to the 'only eat snow that is pure white' rule!

Baby G: Mama, why don't some people celebrate their birthdays?

Summer: Baby G, some people don't like birthdays.

Willie: What is not to like about birthdays? People fuss over you, give you stuff, and you get to eat what you want, carrots. Oh wait, that happens to me every day our park is open. What a life! 😂

Summer: Willie, birthdays are really about celebrating life, not about eating what you want, getting presents, or having a party, although those are nice. Baby, when you are young, every birthday is a big deal. When you are older, you have had a lot of them. Some adults may only want to celebrate the big birthdays.

Willie: All my birthdays are big ones. I am a tall giraffe, and getting bigger all the time, not just on my birthdays! 😂

Baby G: What are the big ones?

Summer: For some adults, a big birthday ends in a zero. So, the big birthdays are the 20th, 30th, 40th, 50th, 60th, 70th, 80th, and if you are lucky, 90th, and if you are very, very lucky, the 100th. For others, big birthdays are those, plus the ones that end in five, the 25th, 35th, 45th, etc. Some people consider every birthday to be a big deal and celebrate every year. People who really like celebrating may celebrate their birthday for a week, or even a whole month! They may attend multiple parties for the same birthday.

Baby G: Why do the ones who don't like birthdays not like them?

Summer: Some don't like a fuss. Some have lost their family, and don't see the point of celebrating their birthday. Some people, that would love to have a celebration, are alone. They have no one to make a fuss over them, so they don't like being reminded that other people do. Some people don't like being reminded that they are getting older. Everyone gets older, you have no say about that. Be glad you made it through another year and are still here. Many people didn't. Even if you don't get presents on your birthday, last year you got the biggest gift of all, another year of life. On your birthday, thank your parents for the gift of life. Baby, today is your nine-month birthday. Happy Birthday!

Baby G: Mama and Daddy, thanks for giving me life.

Summer: You are welcome.

Willie: Wait, I didn't give him Life, I gave him Monopoly. Someone messed up my order. I demand a refund! 🤣

Summer: Willie! Yes, you and I gave him life, and I also thank you for that gift. The world is a better place, because he is in it.

Baby G: World, I hope you celebrate your birthdays. Whether you only celebrate the big ones, celebrate every year, or celebrate the same birthday multiple times, do celebrate the fact you made it through another year. I am glad you are still here!

Baby G: Mama, what are skin and bones?

Willie: Your mama will never be skin and bones. She eats too much. 😂

Summer: Willie, someone who is "skin and bones" is emaciated, very thin, and sick. Baby G, before I answer that, let's do a project together. Our human family will help because we don't have hands. A project is a planned activity, with tasks. It is something you do. It takes time and effort. You create or produce something. A project has a start and an end.

Willie: My project is to build a vacuum system that sucks air. My fans will deposit carrots in one end of a vacuum tube, and I will stand, with open mouth, at the other end. I don't need to be anywhere near my fans. 😂

Summer: Willie! You are sucking the air out of this room. Go do your project and let us do ours. Baby, we are going to make a little giraffe and a little human. Here is a closed plastic bag containing wooden sticks. You cannot touch the sticks, but you can feel that they are there. The bag prevents the sticks from falling out. The bag represents your skin. It protects your insides from the outside world and keeps them from falling out. When you cut your skin by accident, your insides are not protected anymore. You can get an infection, you can get sick. Try not to cut yourself, and if you do, notify your parents, or a teacher, immediately. You may need to see a doctor, or maybe just get a bandage. It imitates skin and protects your insides. Take the cardboard tubes from the inside of two rolls of paper towels. Cut one cardboard tube into three big pieces. Cut one of the big pieces into two. Two big pieces and one of the small pieces will be the "body", "neck" and "head" of the giraffe. Do the same to the other cardboard tube. One big piece and

two small pieces will be the "body", "neck", and "head" of the human. Cut a paper into strips. Wrap and tape strips around the pieces of cardboard to be the "skin". Use tape to join the cardboard pieces together. Push gently on the cardboard pieces, and they will bend a little. The "bodies" need "bones" inside. Bones are rigid, or stiff. Your backbone, or spine, enables you to stay upright. It has parts called vertebrae. Your neck connects your head to the rest of your body. Giraffes and humans have the same number of neck vertebrae, seven, but giraffe vertebrae are much larger than human ones. Neck bones enable you to hold up your head. Leg bones enable you to stand and move. Arm bones enable humans to raise their arms. Giraffes have hooves containing bones, and humans have bones in their hands and feet. Tape wooden sticks inside the "bodies" and "necks" to be "spines" and "neck bones". There are joints between each pair of bones, so you can move. We will use tape "joints". Tape four "legs" to the giraffe "body", and tape two "legs" and two "arms" to the human "body", after wrapping paper "skin" around the "legs" and "arms". Your muscles get energy from food. Then your muscles can move your bones, and your body. You can walk or run or jump. Humans can also hold things. Use your muscles to pretend the little giraffe and little human can move.
Willie: I don't have to pretend that little humans can move. I am a tall bull giraffe, and all humans are little to me.

Watch them move fast when I get too close to them! 😂
Baby G: World, we all have skin, bones, joints and muscles. They keep us healthy, and able to stand and move. But you don't want to be "skin and bones". If you cut yourself, let your parents or a teacher know, so they can take care of you. I don't want you to get sick!

Baby G: Mama, what are haters?
Willie: Ohhhhhhhh, I hate repeat questions! I especially hate repeat questions about hate! 😂
Summer: Willie, some subjects bear repeating. They are important enough to talk about more than once. Besides, to be perfectly accurate, his original question was about hate, and not about haters. We had to talk about haters, while talking about hate.
Willie: Okay, I won't joke anymore today. This subject is too important. Hopefully, you won't hate tomorrow's jokes, or think they are repeats. Maybe, if they are repeats, you'll think they are funny enough to hear more than once. 😂
Summer: Willie, thanks. Baby G, haters are people who hate. But more importantly, they hate it when other people are happy, and they want to take away whatever makes the other people happy.
Baby G: Like what?
Summer: Today, a bunch of haters got together, and made a lot of false reports about our live cam, saying it is bad, when it really isn't.
Baby G: The haters hate us?
Summer: No. They hate that we are captive giraffes, and never mind that we would die in the wild. They hate that our park is a success, and never mind that some of the money raised goes towards helping giraffes in the wild. They even hate the people who watch us. A lot of reports, in a very short time, of supposed bad behavior in a video, or on a live cam, or by the cam owner's channel, makes a company think the video, or the live cam, or the channel, violates that company's rules, when our live cam really didn't. The alleged rule violation generated a bad mark, a strike, against our park's channel. That caused a computer at that company to automatically shut down our live cam for 90 days. People who like to watch us were very upset when the live cam shut down. The live chat shut down too, but it was restored. People chatted about how important the live cam, and the live chat, are to them; how watching us, and chatting about us, teaches them about giraffes; how we distract them from their illnesses, and other troubles; what are their favorite memories of us; how the live cam community impacts their lives, etc. People also chatted about how to make sure the haters didn't win. They found a peaceful way to do that. They started another fundraiser for our park and raised over 1600 dollars in a short time! It took hours before the bogus strike against our park's channel was removed, and our live cam was restored. The world can watch us again.
Baby G: World, fight against the haters, and don't let them win. There are peaceful ways to do that. I am glad you can watch us again!

Willie's Cookbook

Recipe for Making a Baby Giraffe

1 Bull Giraffe
1 Lady Giraffe
Mix Well.
Discard any old baby G's. They are no good.
Add some p.. to taste.

Tasha Poochette

Baby G: Mama, what are recipes?
Summer: Baby G, recipes contain lists of ingredients, and instructions for making something with those ingredients.
Baby G: What are ingredients?
Summer: If it is a food recipe, the ingredients are other foods that you mix together. For example, a carrot cake has carrots in it, along with other ingredients. You need good ingredients to make anything good.
Willie: I have my own cookbook. It has a recipe for making a new baby. You take one bull giraffe and mix it with one lady giraffe. You discard any old baby giraffes. They are not good anymore. Add some p.. to taste. 😂
Summer: Willie! You don't discard old baby giraffes! They are still good! Baby, usually a recipe is for making food, but it can be a recipe for making something else. You follow the recipe carefully, and then you will create something new. It is almost like magic. A pinch of this, a pinch of that, and poof, you make something.
Willie: I'd like a pinch of this, a pinch of that, and a pinch of you, Summer. We can make something happen. 😂
Summer: Willie, giraffes don't have hands, we cannot pinch! We need our human family to help, if we want to cook.
Baby G: What happens if you don't follow a recipe carefully?
Summer: Great cooks don't need recipes. But everyone else needs to follow them carefully. If you don't, that is a recipe for disaster. You won't make anything good, or worth keeping. The people who create recipes have a lot of experience doing that. They test the instructions to make sure other people can follow them. Humans need to eat what is prepared by the cook in their family. If they don't like the food, they shouldn't be forced to eat it. However,

they won't get other food instead. They will have to wait until the next meal to eat.

Baby G: What are meals?

Summer: Each time a reasonably large amount of food is eaten, that is a meal. Smaller amounts of food are snacks. Meals have names. Breakfast is eaten in the morning. Lunch is eaten midday, and dinner is eaten in the evening. In some places, lunch is called dinner, and supper is eaten in the evening. In some places, tea is not just a drink, it is a meal eaten in late afternoon, or early evening. There is an expression, "eat what you cook". It means whatever you expect others to do, you should do too. If you work for, or own, a business, and your company makes something, make sure you use and like your own product.

Willie: I don't eat what I cook. That is because I don't cook food. 😂

Summer: Willie, captive giraffes only eat uncooked food, like hay, carrots, lettuce, etc., or food prepared by our human family, like grain.

Baby G: World, following a food recipe, and creating something new, is fun! Get help from your human family, if you need it. Only use good ingredients and follow the recipe carefully. Eat what you cook, or what the cook in your family makes. What should we make?

Baby G: Mama, what does "too much of a good thing" mean?

Summer: Baby G, a good thing is something that makes you happy, or helps you.

Willie: Carrots are a good thing. I can't get too many carrots. Therefore, too much of a good thing is a good thing. 😂

Summer: Willie, if you eat too many carrots, you will gain weight. Gaining weight is a good thing, while you are still growing up, but it becomes a bad thing, once you are an adult. Baby, sometimes, something that was good is now not good.

Willie: Son, you are a good thing. It makes the world happy to watch you on the live cam. If it is not good to have too much of a good thing, they should shut down the live cam again. 😂

Summer: Willie! The world can never get too much of him! Watching him will never be a bad thing! Baby, that expression, "too much of a good thing", means too much of something that normally is good, or helps you, may actually harm you, or it may make something that was pleasant, unpleasant. For example, prescription medicines, drugs, help you heal, when you are sick or injured, and help get rid of pain. They make you feel better, until you actually are better. They are good things. But if you take too much medicine, or take the wrong medicine for what ails you, the medicine can make you sicker, or even kill you. Too much of a good thing is not good. If you take prescription drugs, when you are not sick, or don't have a prescription, perhaps because you like how they make you feel, you probably will harm yourself, or die. Only take prescription drugs if a doctor tells you, or your parents, that you need the drugs, and only take them for how long the doctor says. Do not give leftover drugs, drugs you still have once you are better, or just feel better, to anyone else. Legal prescription drugs are only legal when a doctor prescribes them for you. As soon as you or someone else abuse them, use them without a prescription from a doctor, or use more of them than you should, they become illegal drugs. Stay away from illegal drugs, and report anyone trying to sell, or give them, to you. Tell someone you trust, like your parents, or a teacher.

Baby G: Are all drugs prescription drugs?

Summer: No, some are "over the counter" drugs. You can buy them in a regular store. You don't need a doctor's prescription. They are not as dangerous as prescription or illegal drugs, but still should not be abused. Some illegal drugs were never prescription drugs. They were created to make the people who buy them addicted to them and make the criminals who sell them rich. Addicts need more and more of those drugs to feel better. They may spend all their money on illegal drugs and turn to crime to get more money. You can't become an addict if you never start using those drugs.

Willie: Yeah, it is better to be a food addict. I am addicted to carrots. I can't get enough! 😂

Summer: Willie, it is better not to be an addict at all. Your life will be so much better.

Baby G: World, use prescription drugs only when a doctor tells you to. Don't use illegal drugs or abuse legal ones.

Don't let too much of a good thing turn it into a bad thing. I want you to get healthy if you are sick, and to stay healthy if you are not sick!

Baby G: Mama, what is a deduction?

Summer: Baby G, a deduction is something you subtract, or remove, from something else.

Willie: I take our son as an income tax deduction. Actually, I wish someone else would just take him! 😂

Summer: Willie, giraffes don't pay taxes! Baby, taxes are the government's share of your income. You must make money to have income, and if you have little income, or no income, you don't have to pay tax on it. A deduction is also something you infer, or figure out, from the facts. You reach a decision, or a conclusion, by thinking about what you know, what the facts are.

Willie: It is not a brilliant deduction, to figure this out: I want more time with your mama; you take up all her time with your endless questions; and if we deduct you from this picture, she'll have more time for me! 😂

Summer: Willie! Figure this out: If you remove him before he must go, I will spend all my time being mad at you! Baby, you will be with us through this coming season, and maybe you and your future mate will stay here forever. I will thoroughly enjoy every minute you are here, and I will not worry about you leaving. I will not worry about the future until it gets here.

Baby G: What deductions can I make?

Summer: Let's set up a situation, a scenario, with some facts. You can use those facts to make some deductions. The world watches us on the live cam. Some people say we are cooped up in too small pens, that we are in jail, and we should be outside, or in the wild. Other people see when both Daddy's and our doors to the outside are open, sometimes we choose to stay in our barn. What does that tell the world?

Baby G: That it is not warm enough outside?

Summer: No. The doors are not opened by our human family unless it is warm enough outside for us to go out. So, if the doors are open, you can deduce that it is warm enough outside. Why shouldn't we be in the wild, where it is warm all the time, instead of being in captivity, where during the winter, it is often too cold to go outside?

Baby G: We are captive giraffes that would die in the wild.

Willie: I want to be wild, not be IN the wild. 😂

Summer: Yes. We want to be both warm AND stay alive. Why do we captive giraffes sometimes choose to stay inside?

Baby G: We like it inside?

Summer: Yes. It is warmer inside. What else can you deduce?

Baby G: People who think our pens are too small, or uncomfortable, are wrong?

Summer: Yes. Our pens are much larger than they appear on the camera, and very comfortable for us. Some people make a bad assumption, that our pens are small, because they look small on the live cam. They draw the wrong conclusion, that our pens are uncomfortable, based on their bad assumption. What else?

Baby G: We are not in jail. We are free to come and go. We choose to be inside.

Summer: Yes!

Baby G: World, it is fun to look at the facts, and make some deductions. But make sure your deductions or conclusions are based on real facts, and not based on assumptions which may be wrong.

Baby G: Mama, what makes things move?

Summer: Baby G, as you know, when you eat, that gives energy to your muscles, and your muscles move your bones, and your body. Some humans and animals have muscles that don't work right. They need help to move. Most animals have muscles, but things that are not alive don't.

Willie: Things cannot eat to get energy. Unless you are talking about "The Thing". 😂

Summer: "The Thing" was not real. It is something in a movie.

Baby G: So, if things cannot eat, and don't have muscles, how do they move?

Summer: An outside force moves them. The wind blows paper around. Your breath blows a soap bubble away from you. If you pick up a rock, and then drop it, gravity makes it fall to the ground. If you use your nose or leg to push an open gate closed, that is an outside force too. But something called friction makes some objects hard to move.

Baby G: What is friction?

Willie: Let me explain that. Fr. is the abbreviation for French. Diction is your choice and use of words. Fr-diction means the French will have choice words for you, if you don't speak French properly. 😂

Summer: Willie! There is no such word as Fr-Diction! Baby, friction is what happens when one surface or object rubs against another. If there is a lot of friction, one surface or object prevents the other from easily moving over it. If there is little or no friction, the second one moves easily over the first one.

Baby G: I don't understand.

Summer: For example, a wooden sled is on a hill. You want the sled to slide down the hill. If the hill has only dirt, it may be hard to get the sled to slide. If the hill has grass on it, it may be a little easier to get the sled to slide. If the hill has snow on it, it is very easy to get the sled to slide. Dirt, grass, and snow cause different amounts of friction.

Baby G: What if you want to use the sled when there is no grass or snow?

Summer: Then you change the friction caused by the sled. You put metal runners on the sled, because metal causes less friction than wood. Or you put wheels on the sled because wheels have very little friction.

Baby G: Can you use a sled with wheels on snow?

Summer: Probably not. The wheels may sink into the snow. Things with wheels run best on hard roads that have been cleared of snow.

Willie: Giraffes may sink into snow. We run best on trails with no snow. Does that mean we are wheels? 😂

Summer: Willie, go try to do a cartwheel, and see if you are anything like a wheel.

Baby G: Is there any other way to reduce friction?

Summer: Yes. Grease, oil, wax, etc. placed between certain objects reduces friction, and makes them easier to move. You could put wax on the metal runners of a sled.

Baby G: World, some things can move on their own, and others need a little help. Watch out for friction, it makes things harder to move.

What Caption?

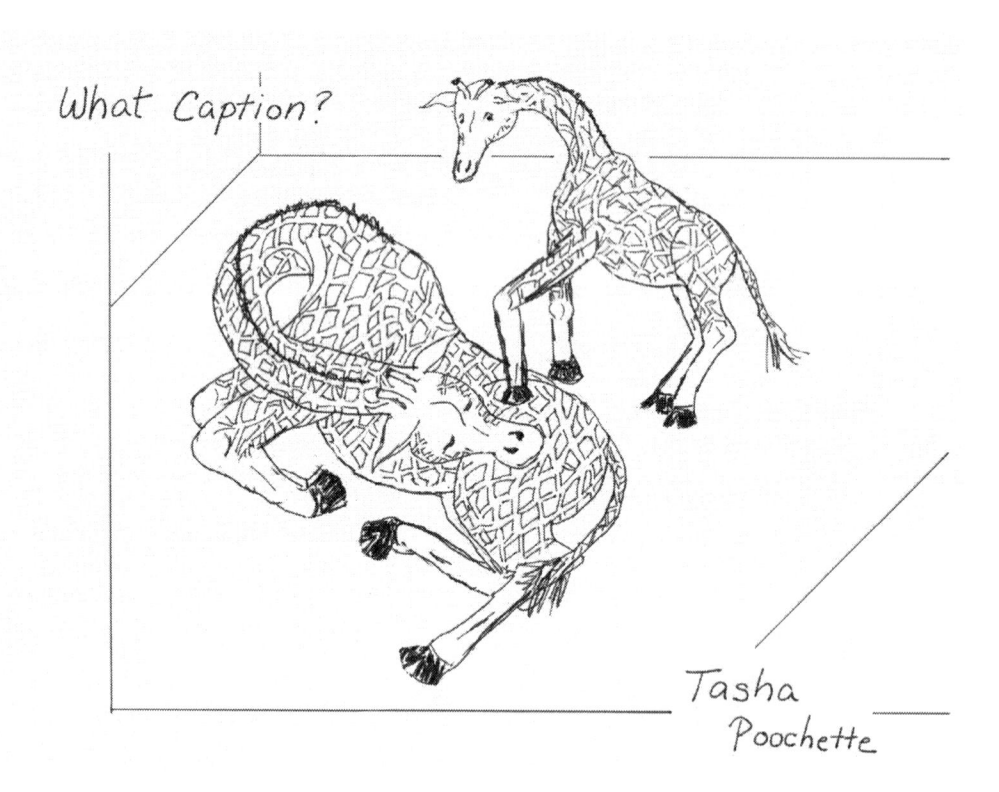

Tasha Poochette

Baby G: Mama, what are captions?

Willie: Cap-G-Tions are giraffes from the Captive Giraffe Nation. They all sing their national anthem a captivella. 😂

Summer: Willie, there is no Captive Giraffe Nation! Captive giraffes live all over the world, in many nations. And that should be "A cappella", which means singing without instrumental accompaniment. There is no music playing in the background. Baby G, when someone lives in a nation, they are called by a name related to their country name. For example, Canadians live in Canada, and Americans, like us, live in the United States of America. Captions are words describing a photo, drawing, painting, video, movie, TV show, etc. They describe what you see. They may include dialogue, what people are saying in a video, movie, or TV show. Closed captions are captions you only see if you turn them on. Open captions are seen by anyone viewing that video, movie, or TV show. Sometimes, captions are called subtitles.

Willie: They should make a movie about our giraffe family, featuring me and my jokes! Maybe, I will win the Best Lead Actor award. They will need a lot of captions, because no human can hear us, even those that hear well. 😂

Summer: Willie! You would be a supporting actor. Our baby would be the star of any such movie! Besides, they would use humans to give us "voices". Captions can be distracting. It takes time and practice to read them quickly, so you can still enjoy the show.

Baby G: Why would someone turn on captions?

Summer: People who don't hear well, or who are deaf, cannot hear all of the dialogue. They can read the captions and know what was said. Even people who do hear well may miss stuff because the background noise, or the music, can drown out the voices. People learning a new language can listen to a show, where everyone is speaking that language, and read captions that are written in their own language.

Baby G: What do captions on photos, drawings, and paintings say?

Summer: They can be factual, saying who or what is the subject, when and where the photo was taken, or when the drawing or painting was created, who created it, etc. Or they can be made up captions, with jokes about the subject. A photo or drawing of me laying down, and you putting your hoof on me, could have a funny caption.

Baby G: Like what?

Summer: It could be anything, the sillier, the better. A meme is an image, video, phrase, or other thing that spreads rapidly on the Internet. It is copied, and often altered in a creative or funny way. Its caption may be changed by a lot of people before they repost that photo, drawing, or other thing.

Willie: If I post a picture of myself, with the caption, "Me! Me!", would that be a meme? 😂

Baby G: World, you can turn on closed captioning, if you need help hearing, or even if you hear well. It makes understanding what was said easier for everyone, including those learning a new language. What silly caption would you put on a photo or drawing of Mama laying down, and my hoof on her?

Baby G: Mama, do all animals have fur?
Summer: Baby G, many, but not all, animals have fur. Humans have hair. Birds have down and feathers. Reptiles have scales. Some animals, like whales, are nearly hairless.
Willie: Whales have blubber, a thick layer of fat. Do you suppose they blubber about being too fat? 😂
Summer: Willie, they don't blubber about their blubber! They are grateful for that fat, it keeps them warm! Baby, to blubber means to cry in a noisy way.
Baby G: What is the difference between fur and hair?
Willie: There must be a difference. Otherwise, those musicals would be called "Fur" and "Furspray", not "Hair" and "Hairspray". 😂
Summer: The word 'hair' is normally used when talking about humans, and the word 'fur' is normally used when talking about animals. Some people say certain breeds of dogs have hair, not fur. They don't know that on the inside, hair and fur are the same. Human hair grows for a longer time (years on their heads, a month or so on their arms and legs), and animal fur grows for a shorter time (months). Hair is often longer and has thinner strands. Fur is usually shorter. It often has thicker strands, and there are usually more strands. Human hair grows mostly on their heads, and animals have fur all over their bodies. Eventually, both hair and fur stop growing, and then strands fall out, they are shed. They leave the body or head, and drop on the ground, or on the furniture. They make a mess. So, people who say their dogs have hair, not fur, are really talking about how long it will be before the hair or fur is shed, and how much hair or fur is shed. Their dogs shed less than other dogs.
Baby G: What are fur, hair, down and feathers, and scales for?

Summer: Animals usually have fur with ground and guard hairs. The ground hairs are soft hairs that keep the animal warm. The guard hairs are coarser hairs that protect the animal against the elements, wind, rain, snow, etc. Human hair keeps their heads warm and looks nice. They often remove hairs from their faces, arms, and legs, because they think that looks nicer. Some males like having hair on their faces. Facial hair is called a mustache, if it is under the nose, and above the mouth, or a beard, if it is on the sides of the face, and on the chin. Humans usually rely on hats and clothes, instead of hair, to keep their heads and bodies warm.

Willie: Yeah, humans are naked apes. The hairy apes shaved the humans' bodies to see what they'd look like without fur and shuddered. They voted the humans out of their tribe. 😂

Summer: Willie! Humans are related to apes, but they weren't voted out of the tribe! Baby, birds fluff out their down and feathers to stay warm. Their feathers enable them to fly. Reptiles warm themselves in the sun. Their scales help them move, protect their bodies, help them retain water, and help them hide. Animals often have whiskers, which are usually long and stiff hairs. When a whisker touches something, it sends sensory information to the animal, telling it about the world, the environment, around the animal.

Baby G: World, whether you have hair, fur, down and feathers, scales, blubber, or you wear clothes, I hope you stay warm.

Baby G: Mama, what does "leave the past behind" mean?
Willie: Son, you are the past baby. I am looking forward to the next one. I am ready to leave the past behind. 😂
Summer: Willie, that is not what "leave the past behind" means! We will never leave our baby behind. New babies don't replace old babies. Baby G, if you keep thinking about the mistakes you made in the past, if you keep dwelling on bad or sad memories, it prevents you from enjoying the present, today. You can't live in the past. It is done, finished. It is better to leave the past behind and think about a better future. Look forward, not back. Yes, you should remember what happened in the past, but don't spend all your time doing that. Learn from your mistakes, resolve not to repeat them, and try to do better. You can make a fresh start.
Willie: I like being fresh with lady giraffes. I leave the old one behind and start fresh with a new one. 😂
Summer: Willie! This old lady giraffe will leave you behind, if you keep on being fresh with other lady giraffes! Baby, a fresh start can mean moving somewhere new, or staying where you are, and starting your life over.
Baby G: I can start my life over? I can be born again?
Willie: Yeah, although it would be hard for your mama to give birth to a ten-foot-tall baby. I bet the world would love to watch THAT. 😂
Summer: Willie, that expression, "born again" doesn't mean you are actually born again. You just do things differently than you did in the past. Baby, long ago, some bad people, convicts, were banished from Great Britain. They were moved on ships to Australia, when it was a jail colony for Great Britain. They started their lives over. They did good things instead of bad things. Now, Australia is a nation full of wonderful people. Today is January 26. The Australians write the date as 26 January. Today, Australians are celebrating Australia Day.
Baby G: World, don't waste your life thinking about the mistakes you made in the past, or about bad or sad memories. Learn from them, leave the past behind, and make a fresh start. Happy Australia Day to the Australians!

Baby G: Mama, can I call someone who is in heaven?
Willie: Sure, you can... if you know their new phone number. It will be something like 1 (800) No such number. 😂

Summer: Willie, there is no phone number for heaven, and no phones there, either! Baby G, if you could call someone who is in heaven, what would you talk about?
Baby G: I never knew my grandma, I would like to chat with her, and ask her what you were like as a child, Mama.
Summer: I don't know, she may still be with us, she may still be alive. Giraffes lose touch with their parents and grandparents, if they are moved. Humans that move from one place to another place can try to stay in touch with their parents, and grandparents. They can write letters, call, text, email, or chat online. They should talk to them about early memories, about the family history, while they are still alive. If someone is already gone, family members and friends can share their memories of that person with each other. Sometimes, they do it on the anniversary of a death, and sometimes, they do it on what would have been the birthday of someone they lost. Nothing stops people from sharing memories all year long. The lady who writes stories about us lost her mama many years ago and loves sharing memories of her.
Baby G: If that lady could call her mama in heaven, what would she talk to her about?
Summer: The lady would tell her mama that even though she has been gone a very long time, she had such a great impact on so many people's lives, she is still sorely missed by many.
Willie: After I am gone, you won't be able to miss me, or my smell. I am a stink bull, and we stink to high heaven. 😂

Baby G: What do other people want to talk to their lost loved ones about?

Summer: Some are curious about God, and life in heaven. Some want confirmation that there is life after death. Others don't believe there is. Some want to know if a loved one is happy at last, and free of pain or discomfort. Are they now able to freely move, see, or hear, if they had disabilities in life? Some want to tell their lost loved ones about their lives now, and about the new people in their lives, like the mates, or children, or grandchildren, the lost person never got a chance to meet. Some want to know if the lost person approves of what they are doing, how they are coping with loss, or how they are behaving.

Willie: I want to know if my lost loved one is not behaving in heaven, are they punished? Do they get time off for good behavior? 😂

Summer: Willie! Giraffes are not punished in heaven or on earth! They don't misbehave. They act according to their true nature, and that is neither good or bad.

Baby G: World, if you lost someone, I am sorry for your loss. If you could call them in heaven, what would you talk about?

Baby G: Mama, what does "once in a blue moon" mean?
Willie: I like to color, using crayons. I use a blue crayon to draw pictures of the moon. Once, on a blue moon, I drew a sad face. It was the Man in the Moon. He was blue. 😂
Summer: Willie, there is no Man in the Moon, the Moon isn't blue, and it isn't sad! Baby G, "once in a blue moon" means something happens rarely, it seldom happens. The second full moon in a month is called a blue moon. It doesn't happen much. The Moon isn't actually a blue color. If you are blue, you are sad.
Baby G: What is a full moon?
Willie: A full moon is when a human drops his pants. Giraffes don't wear clothes, and can't drop their pants, so they can't moon you. Some cartoon ducks wear shirts, but not pants. Maybe, they moon you all the time? 😂
Summer: Willie, go ponder that elsewhere. Baby, the Earth goes around the Sun. The Moon goes around the Earth. The Moon doesn't have its own light. What we call moonlight is really light from the Sun reflected by the Moon. The Moon acts like a mirror. The part of the Moon nearest to the Sun is always lit by the Sun. If the Moon is currently between the Earth and the Sun, we cannot see the lit part of the Moon. The Moon looks dark to us. It is a new moon. If the Moon moves, and we can see part of the lit side of the Moon, it looks like a crescent to us. It is a crescent moon. If the Moon moves more, and we can see all of the lit side of the Moon, it looks round, like a circle. It is a full moon. If the Moon gets brighter each night, it is waxing. If it gets dimmer or darker, it is waning. The different shapes of the Moon are called the phases of the Moon. Every month, the Moon goes through these phases.

Some months, it may go through the full moon phase twice. The second time is called a blue moon.
Baby G: Are there other kinds of moons?
Summer: Yes. As the Moon goes around the Earth, sometimes it is close to the Earth. That makes it look bigger. It is called a supermoon. When the Earth is in the right place between the Sun and the Moon, the Moon will be in the Earth's shadow. That is called a lunar eclipse. The Moon looks reddish. It is called a blood moon. Tomorrow is January 31. Early in the morning, at 4:52 a.m. PST, on the west coast of the USA, there will be a rare "super blue blood moon". The second full moon in the month will look bigger than normal and will be reddish. People who live elsewhere might only see a partial eclipse of the Moon. They can watch videos of it online.
Willie: I live elsewhere, and I want to watch videos online, not of a rare Moon event, but of lady giraffes in the wild. They are getting quite rare, you know. 😂
Summer: Willie! Stop watching other lady giraffes, or your time with me will be not rare, but done! You are right though, lady giraffes, and bull giraffes too, are getting rare in the wild. Their numbers are dropping fast.
Baby G: World, check out the rare super blue blood moon tomorrow. If you cannot see it from where you live, look online for videos of it. Please remember that giraffes in the wild need help, their numbers are dropping fast.

Baby G: Mama, what does "practice makes perfect" mean?
Summer: Baby G, when you do something over and over, you are practicing it. The more times you practice something, the more likely you will get better at doing it. Practice makes perfect. The practice makes it easier for you to do it. Soon, you don't even have to think much about it, you can just do it. People practice playing musical instruments, singing, doing sports like gymnastics, swimming, basketball, baseball, etc. Doctors practice medicine. Newborn baby giraffes practice getting up, standing, balancing, walking, nursing, and laying down. The more they do those things, the better they get at doing them.
Willie: I practice making new babies. My next baby will be named Perfect. Practice makes Perfect. 😂
Summer: Willie, our next baby won't be named Perfect! Anyhow, every baby is perfect to its parents. Even if a baby has some disability, he or she will be loved, despite that disability. Love makes parents ignore any imperfections in their babies.
Baby G: What do I practice?
Willie: You have been practicing your "big boy" moves on your mama. You better not try them on me! 😂
Summer: Willie, he has learned them from watching you! Parents need to be aware their children watch, and may imitate, what the parents do.
Baby G: What do you practice, Mama?
Summer: I practice holding my tongue, not saying anything, when you try those moves. I just move away. I realize you can't actually do anything to me, you are too little. You can only pester me, bother me, and keep me awake. I realize you don't know that you should not make those kinds of moves on your own mama. I realize we are the only giraffes here, so who else could you practice on? Certainly not on your daddy. You really should practice these moves later with your future mate.
Baby G: What should I practice now?

Willie: You should practice stretching your neck. That will make you taller. 😂
Summer: Willie! Stretching doesn't make you taller! Giraffes are tall, because they are born with genes for long legs and long necks. Baby, some things don't change, no matter how much you practice. You need to know what you can change, what you can get better at, and practice that. For example, now that you are taller, it is harder for you to get under me to nurse. But with practice, by spreading your legs, bending your knees, leaning back, bending your neck, etc., you have gotten better at it.
Baby G: World, practice is a good thing because practice makes perfect. However, make sure what you are practicing is a good thing to practice. Sometimes, you need to wait to practice something until you are older, and then practice it with the right person.

Willie's Sundial

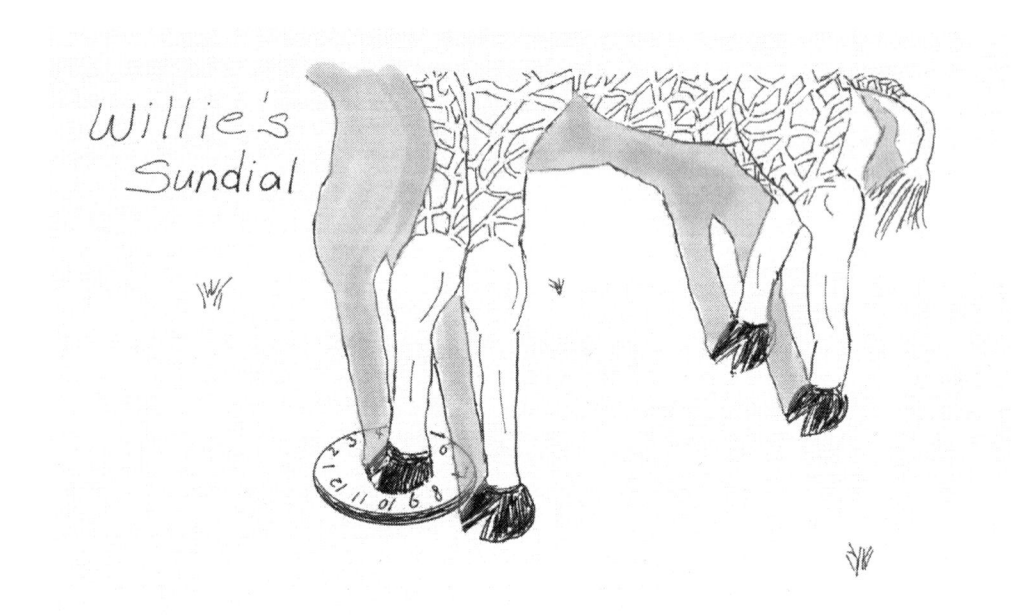

Tasha Poochette

Baby G: Mama, what does it mean to be "afraid of one's own shadow"?

Summer: Baby G, if someone is very timid or nervous, they are afraid to do anything, and they are often scared or frightened, they are said to be afraid of their own shadow.

Willie: I am a bull giraffe. People should be afraid, not of my shadow, but of me! 😂

Summer: Willie, our human family is not afraid of you, they are cautious around you. They don't put themselves between you and where you want to go. Baby, they will be cautious around you too. You will be a big bull giraffe someday. You are already more than one and a half times as tall, and more than three times as heavy as a human. They are not fearful of imaginary dangers. They are cautious, due to real dangers.

Baby G: Is anyone actually afraid of their shadow?

Summer: Young children may be. They don't know their shadows are harmless. Today is February 2, Groundhog Day. If a famous groundhog, Punxsutawney Phil, sees his shadow on Groundhog Day, that means he predicts six more weeks of winter. Another groundhog, Woodstock Willie, does the same thing.

Baby G: Can shadows be used for anything else?

Willie: I am not Woodstock Willie. I don't predict weeks of winter. I am your mama's shadow. I follow her closely. I go where she goes. Then I predict when it is time to make a baby. 😂

Summer: Willie! Stop shadowing me and let us talk. Baby, long ago, before they had clocks and watches, people used sundials to tell time. A shadow on a sundial tells you what time it is.

Baby G: How?

Summer: We can make a sundial. Get your human family to help you cut a piece of cardboard in a circle or use a paper plate. Mark the cardboard or plate with the numbers 1-12, like the numbers on the face of a clock or watch. Cut a little slit in the middle of the cardboard circle or plate. Use something tall and skinny, like a wooden stick, or a pencil, or a straw, as the pointer for our sundial. Push one end of the pointer through the slit into a little foam block. Tape the block to the back of the sundial. Tape other little foam blocks to the back of the sundial to keep it level. When it is warm and sunny outside, hold the sundial. The sunlight will cause the pointer on the sundial to cast a shadow. Use a watch to tell the current time. Turn the sundial around, and, if needed, tilt or slant the pointer, until the shadow points to the current time. For example, if the watch says it is currently 3 p.m., you want the shadow on the sundial to point to the 3. Put the sundial down in that position. As the sun moves, so will the shadow. Later, so long as the sundial is still in the right position, you can use the shadow on the sundial to see what time it is.

Willie: I am tall and have skinny legs. I tried to use my leg as the pointer on my sundial. But my shadow covers the whole thing. I can't tell what time it is. I guess it is time to make a new sundial. 😂

Baby G: World, don't be afraid of your shadow. Don't be afraid of trying something new, or trying something that is actually old, but it is new to you. Even though we can easily use a clock or a watch to see what time it is, it is fun sometimes to do something how people did it long ago. Let's make a sundial!

Baby G: Mama, what is an average?
Summer: Baby G, when you have a bunch of numbers or values, and you add them up, you get a total, a sum. If you divide the sum by how many numbers or values there are in that bunch, you get an average. If your daddy has three carrots, and you have one carrot, and I have two, the total number of carrots is 3 + 1 + 2, or 6. The sum, 6, is divided by 3 because there were three numbers used in that sum (3, 1, 2). So, the average number of carrots is 6 / 3, or 2. We have an average of 2 carrots each.
Willie: See, I knew I was better than average at getting carrots. Our human family loves me more! 😂
Summer: Willie, they don't love you more! You are a bull giraffe, and you are still growing. Our baby is also a bull giraffe, but he is still little, and not yet weaned. He currently gets 20 percent of what his body needs from drinking my milk. I am a full-grown lady giraffe. You need more food than us. Baby, it can be useful to know the average for a group. If you know the average height of a full-grown giraffe, you can make sure, when you build a giraffe barn, that it is tall enough to hold most full-grown giraffes. You should add some extra room, just in case your giraffe ends up taller than the average.
Baby G: What if you want your barn to hold the tallest giraffe ever?
Summer: Then you find out what is the maximum height for a giraffe (over 19 feet including ossicones). You make your barn even taller. A maximum is how much, how big, how tall, how heavy, etc., something can be. The opposite of a maximum is a minimum, how little, how small, how short, how light, etc., something can be. Your daddy has the maximum number of carrots, 3, and you have the minimum number, 1, in our group.
Baby G: What else can you use an average for?
Summer: Recently, a baby Masai giraffe was born. Newborn baby giraffes need to quickly learn how to get up, balance, walk, nurse, and lay down. It took her two hours to stand up, and another half hour to begin to nurse. The average time for a giraffe in captivity, to go from birth to standing up, is an hour. She took a lot longer time

than the average. It took you only about 45 minutes to stand up, less than the average time.
Baby G: Which is better, to take more or less time, than the average?
Summer: It is better to take less time in this case. If she had been on the ground in the wild that long, she probably would not have survived. Lions would've gotten her. Now she is fine and walks and runs around. In other cases, it is better to take more time.
Willie: I take more time than the average giraffe to come up with a joke. That is because the average giraffe doesn't make jokes! 🤣
Summer: Being above average in some things is better than being below average. It is better to get a good grade in school, like an A or a B, than to get an average grade, like a C. If someone has an average appearance, they are not extremely beautiful, or really ugly. If a movie or tv show is average, it is okay, it is not special. Masai giraffes are usually the tallest giraffes. They are taller than the average giraffe.
Willie: I look up at a Masai giraffe. If it is a lady Masai giraffe, I look her up and down. 😂
Summer: Willie! Stop eyeing other lady giraffes, or I will give you a bigger than average cold shoulder!
Baby G: World, don't aim to be just average. Try to stand out.

Baby G: Mama, what does it mean to set a record?

Summer: Baby G, as you already know, a record can be a document, such as a birth record, a pet record, or a historical record. It can also be a recording, where a sound, someone's voice, or some music, is put on a tape, a vinyl record, a compact disc, a streaming music player, a computer, or something else.

Willie: I made voice recordings of some of my jokes. I recorded them on a vinyl record. No one can hear those jokes, because they don't have record players anymore. 😂

Summer: Willie, some humans still have record players. They like the sound better than what they hear when they use digital music players, or computers. Even though some humans still have record players, humans cannot hear your record, because humans can't hear giraffes! Baby, computers may store information, data, in records. The important thing is having a record of something, whether on paper, or in a recording, or on a computer, means you can go back later, and look at or hear it. It helps you remember what happened. You can still play and hear recorded songs and music, when the singer or musician is somewhere else, or after they are gone.

Willie: I like to keep records of which of my fans gave me the most carrots, so I can go back later to just that fan and get more! 😂

Summer: Willie! If you go back to every fan, you'll get the most carrots. A little from a lot of people is usually more than a lot from just one person. Baby, you can be almost sure something has never happened before if there is no record of it. Of course, some things happened so long ago, they happened before people or computers started keeping records. There are things in nature, like the fossil record, that help us understand what happened back then. Plus, if you are not careful, your records could be incomplete, or inaccurate. Maybe you didn't record everything that happened, or you wrote down the wrong thing. You may falsely think something never happened, or that it happened a different way than it really did, if you have bad, wrong, or incomplete records. If you keep good, accurate, and complete records, you can search them, and see if someone just did something that has never been done before. If so, they set a record.

Willie: I set a record for making the most new jokes every day. No other giraffe can keep up with me. Of course, they aren't trying to keep up. Other giraffes don't make jokes.

Summer: Willie, go think of some more jokes elsewhere. Let us talk. Baby, maybe they did something no one has done before, or maybe they did something faster, or longer, or better than anyone ever did it before. Maybe they ate more of something, like hot dogs, in a shorter time than anyone's ever done before.

Baby G: World, keep good, accurate, and complete records. It is good to know what happened before now. It is fun to set a new record, do something faster, or longer, or better than anybody did before. What should we try to do?

Baby G: Mama, why do camels have humps?
Summer: Baby G, a camel has one or two humps. A camel hump contains a big mound of fat.
Willie: If you call a camel fat, are you complimenting it, or are you insulting it? 😂
Summer: Willie, you shouldn't comment on anyone's weight! Baby, the stored fat in a camel's hump acts like food, and gives the camel energy, when there is little actual food to eat. The camel can go without eating actual food, like plants, grass, grains, or hay, for up to three weeks. As the fat in the camel's hump is used, the hump starts to sag, and flops over to one side.
Willie: If I went three weeks without food, all of me, not just my hump, would flop over to one side! 😂
Summer: Willie! Giraffes don't have humps! They need to eat every day. Baby, there is no water in the camel's hump. The camel can go for seven days without drinking water, because its blood and its organs, its kidneys and intestines, are so good at retaining, and using water. Very little water is wasted. When the camel does drink water, it can drink up to twenty gallons of water, or about 76 liters, at a time. That is a lot of water!
Baby G: How much water do giraffes drink?
Summer: Giraffes in the wild get most of their water from the plants and leaves they eat, such as acacia leaves. Giraffes can actually go without drinking water longer than camels can! It is awkward for a giraffe to spread its legs, lower its neck, and drink water. They only do it once every few days. They can drink up to 10 gallons, or 38 liters, of water at a time.
Baby G: What are organs?

Summer: Inside your body, along with your muscles and bones, you have various organs that cooperate, work together, to process food and liquids. Other organs move your blood and enable you to breathe. Your organs do these things to keep you alive, and to give your body energy. Remember, your muscles need energy to move your bones.

Baby G: Why do some camels have two humps?

Willie: They are smart. They have a hump to use now, and a spare to use later. I am smart too. I want to make a new baby. Then I'd have an heir, and a spare! 😂

Summer: Willie, spare us from your jokes. Go away and let us talk. Baby, they are Bactrian camels from Asia. The camels with one hump are Arabian camels. They are also known as dromedary camels. Baby camels don't have humps until they start eating solid foods, like hay.

Baby G: Do they say Happy Hump Day when they finally get their humps?

Summer: Today is Wednesday. It is often called Hump Day. People who work from Monday to Friday are halfway done with their work week on Wednesday. So, they are over the hump on Wednesday. Wish them a Happy Hump Day.

Baby G: World, check out camels! They can go for days without eating food or drinking water. But when it comes to not drinking water for a long time, we giraffes have camels beat! If you work during the week, Happy Hump Day!

Lady
Giraffe
On Ice

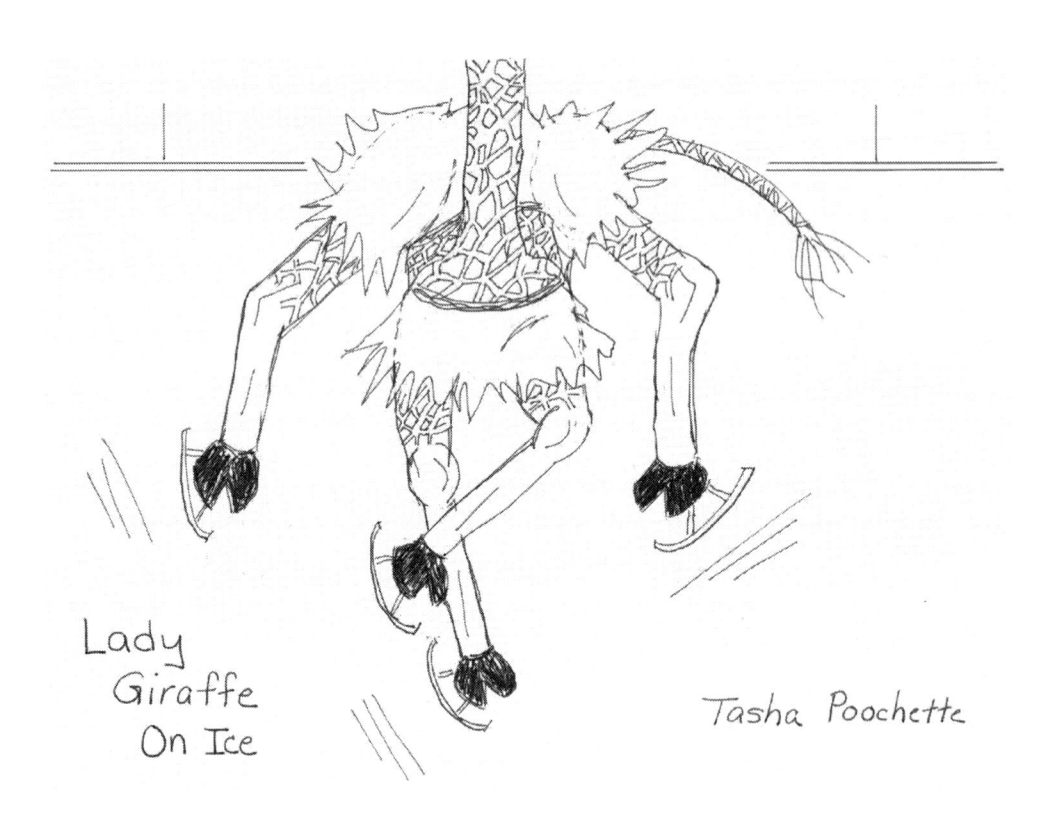

Tasha Poochette

Baby G: Mama, what is anticipation?

Willie: I had an aunt named Cipation. She was so eager to get to her future, she'd put the cart before the giraffe, and never get anywhere. We called her Auntie Cipation. 😂

Summer: Willie, you never had an aunt named Cipation! And that expression is "put the cart before the horse". Giraffes don't pull carts! The cart should be put behind the horse. Baby G, that expression, "put the cart before the horse" means you are putting something, or doing something, in the wrong order. When you anticipate something, you are excited about something that will happen in the future. You look forward to it happening. You are eager for it to happen. You wait in anticipation for it.

Baby G: Like what?

Willie: I anticipate the return of my fans when our park reopens in the spring. I will be taller then. That means I can be further away from my fans, yet still get their carrots. 😂

Summer: Willie! Don't be so obvious about how you don't want to be near your fans, and how you only want them near you until you can grab their carrots. They might feel used, and stop giving you what you want, since you don't give them what they want, time with you. Baby, if you ask someone to be your mate, you wait in anticipation for them to say they will. If you are told you get to go somewhere you really want to go, or you get to go on a trip, you wait in anticipation, until it is time to go. If there is a show or event you really want to see, you look forward to it, with anticipation. You may anticipate hearing someone sing a song, or hearing a musician play your favorite kind of music. You may anticipate learning about a subject that interests you or learning a new skill.

Baby G: What do you anticipate, Mama?

Summer: I enjoy watching the Winter Olympic Games on TV. They start soon. I anticipate watching them, because I have watched them in earlier years, and I know I will enjoy watching them now.

Baby G: What are the Olympics?

Willie: I like watching lady giraffes participate in the Olympic ice skating events. Their skirts look so short, because their legs are so long. 😂

Summer: Willie, giraffes can't ice skate! Baby, giraffes cannot even walk on ice, which is why we must stay in our barn, if there is even a chance of icy conditions outside. Lady humans wear ice skating costumes, which do have short skirts, but they also wear tights that cover their legs. I will tell you about the Olympics tomorrow. You can anticipate learning about them.

Baby G: World, it is fun to look forward to doing, watching, hearing, or learning something you know you will enjoy. What do you anticipate doing, or watching, or hearing, or learning, in the future?

Baby G: Mama, what are the Olympics?

Willie: If you take pictures of someone's swollen lymph glands, they will say, "Oh, lymph, pics!" 😂

Summer: Willie, go take pictures elsewhere. Baby G, when you play sports, it is fun to compete against other people in your town or city. You can compete either as an individual, by yourself, or as a member of a team. If you or your team are good enough, you can compete against other people in your state, or even in other states. If you are very good, you can compete to see who is the best at your sport in your country. If you are great, you can compete to see who is the best in the world at doing your sport. You can represent your country at a worldwide competition.

Willie: I am the best in the world at being me. No one can be better at being me than me. There is no competition. 😂

Summer: Willie, that is sort of true. No one can be better at being you than you, but they shouldn't try. They should realize no one is better at being THEM than them and try to be the best version of themselves they can be. Baby, every four years, the best of the best compete at the Olympic Games. The Olympic Games include most, but not all, sports. The Summer Olympics have warm weather sports, like running and swimming, and the Winter Olympics have cold weather sports, like skiing and ice skating. The Summer Olympics and the Winter Olympics used to be held in the same year, but now are staggered on different four-year cycles. The 2018 Winter Olympic Games officially start today. Countries, that normally may fight each other, agree to stop fighting long enough to peacefully compete. Everyone wants to see who the best of the best in the world is, who can go faster, who is stronger, who can go higher, and who can go longer. They cheer when an individual, or a team, from their own country gets a gold, silver, or bronze medal. The national anthem for the winner's country is played when they get their medal. Some people cheer for anyone from anywhere, not just from their own country, if that person shows what can be done with talent, skill, and hard work. Some people set Olympic records in their sports.

Baby G: Why are they called the Olympics?

Summer: Long ago, in Olympia, Greece, they competed in a 200-meter (222 yard) foot race. The ancient Greeks believed in a king of the gods, named Zeus, who supposedly lived on Mt. Olympus. The foot race was done in his honor. Later, other sports were added. Much later, the modern Olympics included people from many countries, not just Greece, and many more sports.

Baby G: Does everyone watch every competition?

Summer: No. There are too many competitions, in too many sports, with too many people, teams, and countries competing, to watch everything. Choose what competitions you want to watch, decide what sports you enjoy, and watch just those.

Willie: I just want to watch lady giraffes compete for my attention. 😂

Summer: Willie! If you keep watching other lady giraffes, I will break the Olympic record for "how fast and how far can a heavy bull giraffe be tossed out"?

Baby G: World, let's watch the Winter Olympic Games. Cheer for the people and teams from your country, and for anyone from anywhere, who shows what can be done with talent, skill, and hard work. What sports do you want to watch?

Baby G: Mama, what are cents?

Summer: Baby G, the prefix cent- means a hundred. A century is a hundred years. In the United States, and some other places, money is counted in dollars. A dollar bill is worth a hundred cents. Both can buy the same things. A cent is the same as a penny. The US penny coin is made of copper and other metals. The coins used in the USA are pennies (worth 1 cent), nickels (5 cents), dimes (10 cents), quarters (25 cents), half dollars (50 cents), and dollar coins (100 cents). Dollar coins are not as common as dollar bills.

Willie: It would not make sense for you to swap two hundred cents for my one-dollar bill, but it would make cents for me to make that deal. 😂

Summer: Willie, don't take advantage of your son's lack of knowledge! You should protect him, from those who want to take advantage of him, until he knows enough to protect himself. Baby, think before deciding how or when to spend your cents or dollars. It is fun to think about what you want, before you have enough money to get it. Save some of your money, don't spend it all. Some kids put their cents, and other money, in piggy banks.

Willie: I tried to put money in my pig. He went, "Oink, oink". Then he went away. I guess he doesn't like eating money. 😂

Summer: Willie! Piggy banks are not real pigs! And that expression, "eating money", means something is expensive, or it wastes money, not that it really eats money. Baby, grownups put their money in regular banks. They save their money, until they have enough to buy what they want. People with little money "count the pennies". That expression means they are careful about how much they spend. Money is different in different countries. In the UK, they have pounds instead of dollars. They say, "Take care of the pennies and the pounds will take care of themselves". That means if you keep saving small amounts of money, you will soon have large amounts of money. It also means if you take care of little things, they can add up to big things.

Willie: I take care of the little carrots, and the pounds add up. Those are pounds of weight, not UK money. 😂

Summer: Willie, go lift some weights, and you'll soon get rid of that extra carrot weight. Let us talk. Baby, some countries have pictures or drawings of Kings or Queens on their money. Most of the coins and bills in the USA have drawings of former Presidents. The penny has a drawing of President Lincoln. Today is his birthday. He was born on February 12, 1809. Had he lived, he would now be 209 years old!

Baby G: World, think about saving some of your money. It is fun to think about what you want to get, once you have saved enough money. Happy 209th Birthday, President Lincoln!

Baby G: Mama, what are special anniversaries?
Summer: Baby G, as you know, an anniversary is something that happens once a year. Every anniversary is important.
Willie: Once a year, I try to remember my anniversary. But because it happens only once a year, I forget when it is. If I ask your mama to tell me when it is, she gets mad at me. Then I forget why she is mad at me and ask her. That makes her even madder. 😂
Summer: Willie, part of caring for your mate is remembering when your anniversary is. If you cannot remember, ask once, and write it down! Baby, some anniversaries are special. They are the first anniversary, and the fifth, the tenth, and every five years afterwards. The 25th, 50th, 60th, and 75th are extra special anniversaries. The first anniversary is called the paper anniversary. The fifth anniversary is wood. The tenth anniversary is tin. The 25th is silver, the 50th is gold, the 60th is diamond, and the 75th is platinum or diamond, depending on where you live.
Baby G: What about the 100th?
Summer: It all depends on what kind of anniversary we are talking about. There are wedding anniversaries, the anniversary of the birth of a country, the anniversary of when a King or Queen was crowned, the anniversary of when something happened, etc. Very few people live to a hundred, but yes, since a birthday is an anniversary too, some people do celebrate their 100th anniversaries. There are also anniversaries of when something began.
Baby G: Like what?
Summer: For example, last weekend was the anniversary of when people started watching us on the live cam. Our fans have watched your daddy and me for a year and watched you for almost ten months. People call it a "cam-iversary".

Willie: I figure turnabout is fair play. I turned the camera, so we can see our fans. Turns out they are tortoises. 😂

Summer: Willie! Our fans are not tortoises! You don't understand how the live cam works. Our fans are not standing behind the live cam. Whatever it is pointed at, whatever it is focused on, like the tortoises in the loft, it records. Those recorded images or videos are sent to a computer. The computer stores the recordings, so that the world can use their devices to view the videos right then or later. Baby, that expression, "turnabout is fair play", means you had your turn, and now I get my turn. It also means if you hurt me, or you do something to me, I get to hurt you, or do something to you. It is better to stick with the first meaning, and take turns doing something good. Try not to retaliate when someone harms you. Tell someone you trust about what happened.

Baby G: Will the world be able to watch me if I go somewhere else to be with my future mate?

Summer: Our human family says you will be here at least through the 2018 season, and maybe forever. If you must leave, I hope your new barn will have a live cam. Then your fans can still watch your daddy and me, and also watch you and your future mate. You can still be a live cam star!

Willie: Yeah, if you have your own live cam, your mom and I can shut down our live cam temporarily, and have a little privacy, while we make a new live cam star! 😂

Baby G: World, Happy Cam-iversary. I hope you continue watching us for years to come. If I go somewhere else to be with my future mate, I hope you can follow me there, and watch my family grow.

Summer's Valentine's Day gift, lost in the mail for two months

Willie
U.S.A.

Summer
U.S.A.

Baby G
Live Animal

Live!
Handle with care

Dear Postal Customer, we are sorry for the delay...

Tasha Poochette

Baby G: Mama, what is a labor of love?
Willie: It takes a lot of work, or labor, to come up with my jokes. But I love being famous, so it is a labor of love. 😂
Summer: Willie, you should make jokes because you love doing it, not just to be famous. Baby G, a labor of love is something you do, not for money, or fame, or any other benefit, but because you enjoy doing it, or you do it for someone else's benefit, or enjoyment. You volunteer to do it, no one forces you to do it. You get no reward for doing it, yet you do it anyway.
Baby G: Was it a labor of love when you had me?
Summer: Oh yes! I didn't do it to become famous. I became famous after the fact. I did it because the number of giraffes in the wild is dropping rapidly. Every captive giraffe does their part to fight against giraffes going extinct and disappearing from the world.
Willie: I do my part to fight against one giraffe, me, from going extinct. I eat as many carrots as I can. The only thing disappearing from here is my waistline. 😂
Summer: Willie! Disappear from here, leave us, and let us talk. Baby, if they can have children, they do. If they cannot, or they are too young or too old, they still can teach the world about giraffes.
Baby G: I love teaching the world about giraffes and inviting them to share my journey. What else can I do to show the world I love them?
Summer: You can create a Valentine's Day card for them. Today is February 14. It is Valentine's Day.
Baby G: What is Valentine's Day about?
Summer: Valentine's Day is a holiday celebrating love. If you love someone, you can create or buy a card for them, and ask them to be your Valentine. You can give them gifts

or candy or flowers. You can give Valentine's Day cards to many people, if you want, so they won't feel left out. Kids often give cards to all the other kids in their class. You should show love to everyone all year, but on Valentine's Day, make an extra effort to include people who are alone.

Baby G: Can I ask the whole world to be my Valentine? I love them all, and don't want anyone to feel left out, or alone!

Summer: Yes, baby, you can. The world will love that.

Willie: It is no joke, I love you, Summer. I even love the little bull giraffe that finally showed up here almost ten months ago. He was supposed to be your Valentine's Day gift, but he got lost in the mail for two months. 😂

Summer: Willie, he wasn't lost in the mail! Babies are born when they are ready to be born, not on a schedule.

Baby G: World, will you be my Valentine? I am making a card. It is for all of you. I don't want anyone to feel left out. Shhhhh, don't tell my mama and daddy, but I am making cards for them too, because I love them. Happy Valentine's Day!

Baby G: Mama, what are special birthdays?

Summer: Baby G, every monthly birthday is important, until you are a year old. Every yearly birthday for your whole life is important. The special birthdays occur when you are 1, 13, 15, 16, 18, 21, 35, 55, or 65 years old. Extra special ones occur when you are 75, 80, 90 and 100 years old.

Baby G: Why are they special birthdays, or extra special ones?

Willie: All my yearly birthdays are extra special. I have had only six of them. Anything that rare is extra special. Also, I am a giraffe comedian, which is extremely rare. Isn't that special? 😂

Summer: Willie, you are especially focused on yourself. Baby, your first yearly birthday is special, because it is your first. Your thirteenth birthday is special, because you leave your childhood, and enter your teens. You become a teenager. Depending on where you live, and what religion you practice, at different ages, you stop being a child, and become a young man or woman. You come of age.

Willie: I came of age, but I became a young bull, not a young man. At what age will I stop being a giraffe, and become a human? 😂

Summer: Willie! Giraffes don't ever become humans! Baby, the words "man" and "woman" don't just refer to male and female humans. They also refer to age and maturity.

Baby G: What is maturity?

Summer: When you are physically mature, your body is fully grown. You are as tall as you will ever be, you can make babies, etc. When you are mentally and emotionally mature, you accept adult responsibilities. If you are human, you work to earn money, and you pay for your own food, and your home. If you have children, you support them. You don't rely on your parents to pay for everything. You take care of yourself and your family. You understand the consequences, the results, of what you do, you stay calm in serious situations, and you act like an adult.

Willie: I may get older, but I refuse to grow up! I wanted to run away and join Peter Pan in Neverland. The only problem was he said "Never!". They say that word a lot in Neverland. 😂

Summer: Willie, that is a fictional place in a story. In real life, you must grow up, but you still can look at the world with wonder, like a child, forever. Baby, Jews have religious ceremonies, called a bar mitzvah, for a boy when he turns 13, and a bat mitzvah, for a girl when she turns 12 or 13. In some places, when a girl turns 15, she has, or becomes, a quinceañera. In other places, when you turn 16, you celebrate your sweet 16. You are old enough to get a driver's license. In the USA, and some other places, legally you are an adult at age 18. You can vote, sign a contract, own property, decide where to live, what to do, etc. You no longer need your parent's permission to do things. In other places, you are legally an adult at age 21. At age 35, in the USA, you can ask people to vote for you to be President. At 55, you celebrate your "double nickel" birthday. Some people stop working and enjoy early retirement at 55. At 65, almost everyone retires. The 75th, 80th, 90th and 100th birthdays are extra special, because not everyone gets to live that long. Today is your ten-month birthday. Happy Birthday Baby G.

Baby G: World, every birthday is important, but some are special. I hope you enjoy all your special birthdays, and you live long enough to enjoy all your extra special ones.

Baby G: Mama, what is a moment of silence?

Summer: Baby G, when everyone is quiet for a minute, when no one makes a sound for a minute, that is called a moment of silence.

Willie: I want many moments of silence from you, and an end to your endless questions. I have a question of my own. Can something that is endless actually end? 😂

Summer: Willie, that is not what a moment of silence is for. I welcome all his questions, and even yours.

Baby G: What is it for?

Summer: After a tragedy, people respect and honor the victims, the injured, and the dead, and support their families, by having a moment of silence.

Baby G: What is a tragedy?

Summer: If something happens, where people are hurt or killed, or buildings or other things are destroyed, like in a serious accident, or because of a natural disaster, that is a tragedy. It is also a tragedy, if a bad person deliberately harms or kills people. A play or a movie, with an unhappy ending, or where the main character meets with disaster, is also called a tragedy.

Baby G: What do people do during a moment of silence?

Summer: Usually, they stop whatever they were doing, and pray. If they don't believe in prayer, they just wait in silence. Sometimes, if they live near where the tragedy occurred, they bring flowers there. They bring toys if the victims were children.

Willie: Okay, I will stop joking for a moment, and pray for the lost children and adults. They didn't and don't deserve any of this. 😢

Summer: Thanks, Willie. Baby, before, during, or after the moment of silence, people may attend a candlelight vigil in honor of the victims. They hold lit candles. They don't sleep. Instead, they keep watch, or pray for the dead, or talk about what happened, or talk about the victims. They mourn the victims.

Baby G: What else can they do?

Summer: They can resolve to never be the cause of tragedy themselves and teach their children to never be the cause either. If the tragedy was caused by a bad guy, he is caught and punished. But unfortunately, that won't bring back the dead. We need to prevent tragedies in the first place. If you see someone planning a tragedy, say something about it to someone you trust. Don't worry about being a tattletale or being called names. If they don't understand why what they are planning is wrong, or they need help to understand, let's get them help, and avoid tragedies. Tragedies due to accidents, or due to natural disasters, cannot be avoided, but maybe other tragedies can be prevented.

Willie: It would be a tragedy to not prevent a tragedy if you know it is coming. 😢

Baby G: World, hold a moment of silence, or attend a vigil. Mourn the victims of a tragedy. Don't be the cause of one. Say something if you see something. Help others to understand that they shouldn't cause tragedies either.

Baby G: Mama, what is the difference between a president and a President?

Willie: That is Obvious, with an uppercase O. One has a little p, and the other has a big P. Speaking of a little p.., 😂

Summer: Willie, we aren't speaking of that! Besides, you should not ridicule someone for not knowing something. Help them learn. Baby G, the uppercase, or big P, and the lowercase, or little p, are two forms of the same letter. The word President has an uppercase P as its first letter. It has been capitalized.

Baby G: Why was it capitalized?

Summer: Some countries, not all, elect their leaders. It is customary to refer to the elected leader of a country as its president. If you refer to the leader by name, you use the title President, with a capital P, in front of his or her name.

Baby G: Are other words capitalized?

Summer: You should capitalize the first word in a document or in a sentence. You should capitalize the names of people, places, or things. You should capitalize titles that are used before names. A title is something like president, senator, judge, etc. Don't capitalize jobs that are used before names. A job is something like director or coach. Do capitalize titles, roles, or nicknames that are used in place of a name. For example, use Mama, with a capital M, when asking me a question. There are more capitalization rules, but you can learn about them later. Today is Presidents Day in the USA. Given what you now know, what do you think it means? What are we celebrating?

Baby G: It is Presidents Day with a capital P. It celebrates the leader of our country?

Summer: The first president of our country was President Washington. You have heard about President Lincoln. We used to celebrate their birthdays separately. Now we celebrate all U.S. presidents, past and present, on Presidents Day.

Baby G: What if someone doesn't like the current president, or doesn't like what an earlier president did or said?

Willie: I don't know who is, or was, president, or what they did or said. How do I know if I don't like them, or what they did or said? 😂

Summer: Willie! Learn history and read or watch the news. Baby, it doesn't matter if you like or dislike them, or what they did or said. You are honoring the fact every U.S. president has been peacefully elected since the beginning of our country. You are honoring our system of government, which is a constitutional democratic republic. It is also called a representative democracy. We elect representatives and senators to make our laws. We don't vote on every law ourselves. We elect the president to carry out our laws and direct the federal government.

Willie: I am glad they do all that work, as I am too busy eating carrots to do it. 😂

Summer: Willie, it is your job to make time to vote. Choose your representatives, senators, and president carefully. Choose them based on what they think, what they have done, and what they will do for our country, not on what they look like, or on their personalities.

Baby G: World, today is Presidents Day, with a capital P, in the USA. I am glad we have peacefully elected presidents. Happy Presidents Day!

Baby G: Mama, can we have our own Olympics?

Summer: Baby G, yes, we can. Usually, males compete with males, and females compete with females. Males are typically stronger and bigger than females, so it is not fair for males to compete with females. Only in events like shooting, where strength and size are not important, do males compete with females. Of course, in pair events, like ice skating pairs, each pair has one male and one female. We are the only giraffes here, so we will let you and Daddy, two males, compete with a female, me. We need to have competitions that are suited to our talents. What can giraffes do really well?

Willie: Bull giraffes are really good at the mating pairs competition. We match the ladies, move for move. We walk backwards and block the ladies from leaving the area. 😂

Summer: Willie, if you don't leave the area now, and let us talk, you'll quickly discover my secret. I have been letting you think you can block me and keep me from leaving. You really can't.

Baby G: We can run really fast.

Summer: Okay, we can have a sprint race. Whoever finishes first is the winner, and gets the gold medal, the second-place finisher gets the silver medal, and the third-place finisher gets the bronze. There are only three of us here, so we all get medals.

Willie: In a carrot eating competition, if I finish my portion first, and then finish off your portion, and your mama's portion too, do I get all three medals? I am a glutton for medals, they are shiny and glittery. 😂

Summer: Willie! That would mean you are simply a glutton, not that you would get all three medals. The winner gets only the gold medal, and only the winner gets the gold medal. Baby, in real life, not everyone gets a medal, or even something that says they participated. Sometimes, you participate just for the joy of it, because it is fun. Or you want to see how well you can do against others, and you try to do better the next time. The important thing is not to beat someone else, it is to do better this time than you did last time. You are really competing with yourself. We giraffes can also run for a long time and run a long way. We will have a marathon event, where you run over a long distance, 26.2 miles, which is 26 miles and 385 yards (42.195 kilometers).

Baby G: Why that distance?

Summer: The modern marathon was inspired by a story about an ancient Greek messenger who ran from Marathon to Athens, a distance of almost 25 miles. Later, at the request of a Queen of England, it was extended to the current distance. What else can giraffes do well?

Baby G: We can kick very well.

Summer: We will have a game of soccer, which in other countries is called football. Here in the USA, football is a different game than soccer. When you play soccer, you kick a ball towards a goal, and score points if the ball goes past the goalie. You can't use your hands, but you can use your head to bump the ball.

Willie: Whatever you call it, giraffes are good at it. It doesn't matter to us that we cannot use hands that we don't have. 😂

Baby G: World, I hope you are enjoying watching the Olympics. You can have your own Olympics. What events do you want to have? What do you do really well? What would be fun to do? Try to do better this time than last time.

Baby G: Mama, what are alternatives?
Summer: Baby G, when you have two or more ways to do something, you have choices or alternatives. You choose one. If one way doesn't work out, you can try an alternative way.
Baby G: Like what?
Willie: I want to go to Cheyenne Mountain Zoo and meet with the lady giraffes. If having my way with one doesn't work out, I can try an alternative one. 😂
Summer: Willie! If you choose to do that, you leave me no alternative, you will be on your way out of here! Baby, if you walk along a road, and there is a fork in the road, you can choose between two alternatives.
Willie: I say, choose to pick up the fork, and eat. I am starving! 😂
Summer: Willie, giraffes don't use forks and spoons to eat! Besides, a fork in a road isn't an eating utensil. The road splits, and one path goes to the left, and one path goes to the right. You choose between taking the path to the left or taking the one to the right. Baby, your body has a pretend line between the top of your head and your tail. Everything on one side of the line is on your left side. Everything on the other side of the line is on your right side. So, you have a left ear, a left front leg, and a left back leg. You also have a right ear, a right front leg, and a right back leg. Humans don't have tails and stand upright. They have two ears, two legs and two arms. The line goes from the top of their head to their feet. So, they have a left ear, a left arm, and a left leg. They also have a right ear, a right arm, and a right leg. They have a left hand, and a right hand. If they prefer to use their right hand to do things like writing, they are right-handed. Otherwise, they are left-handed.

Baby G: Does everything have alternatives?
Summer: No. Sometimes, you have no choices, there are no alternatives. But many things do have alternatives.
Baby G: Is there an alternative to the Olympics?
Summer: Yes. If you are physically disabled, there is something wrong with your body, but you may still be able to do sports. Maybe you can do sports with help, like with an artificial leg, an artificial arm, or some other man-made body part. If you are good enough, you can participate in the Paralympics. The Paralympic Games are held after the Olympics at the same location. If you are mentally disabled, there is something wrong with your brain, or if you have certain physical disabilities, you can participate in the Special Olympics. If you are or were in the U.S. military, serving our country, and you are or were wounded, injured, or ill, you can participate in the Warrior Games. If you served anywhere, and you are or were wounded, injured, or ill, you can participate in the international Invictus Games.
Willie: I prefer to participate in the Inhale-It Games, where you eat as much as you can, before taking a breath. You inhale your food. 😂
Baby G: World, you have many choices, and many alternatives. Even if you have a disability, or need help, there is an alternative that still allows you to compete and have fun.

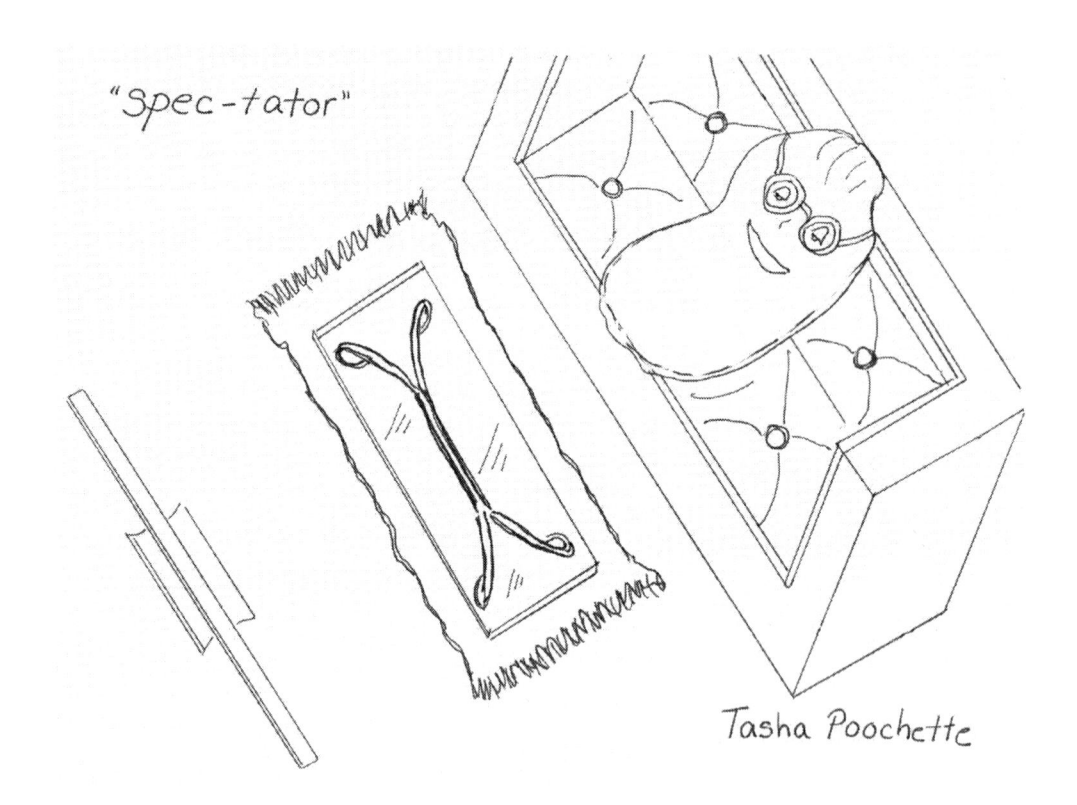

"Spec-tator"

Tasha Poochette

Baby G: Mama, what is a spectator?
Willie: A potato is often called a tator. A potato wearing spectacles is a spec-tator. A couch potato wearing spectacles is a special kind of spec-tator. 😂
Summer: Willie, potatoes don't wear spectacles! And that word is tater, not tator. Baby G, a couch potato is a human who spends a lot of time sitting or lying on a couch and watching a lot of TV. A spectator is someone who watches or observes things, like sporting events. They may watch in person, or watch TV, videos, or movies. They watch instead of participating.
Baby G: Which is better, to watch, or to participate?
Summer: It depends on what we are talking about. We watch the Olympics. We cannot participate. Most people cannot participate. It takes a lot of talent, skill, and hard work, to get to the Olympics. Before you can compete there, you must train. Often, you must travel to train with experienced coaches. You must travel to compete with other people from your country, who also would like to get to the Olympics. Not everyone who competes gets to go. Only the best do. All of that, training, traveling, and competition, takes money. People with little or no money need sponsors who can pay for what they cannot. Some, who have the talent and skill, and who are willing to work hard, but have no money or sponsors, don't get the opportunity to compete. It is sad, but sometimes life is sad.
Willie: I want sponsors to pay for more lady giraffes to live here and compete for my attention, but your mama won't let me ask for money for that project. It is sad. 😂
Summer: Willie! If you get other lady giraffes to move in, I will ask for sponsors to pay for me to move out! Baby, when you can participate in something, it is often better

than just watching. Don't just watch TV, or just watch videos on a computer or phone. Don't be a spectator all your life.

Baby G: What does that mean?

Summer: If someone invites you to dance, don't worry about looking foolish, please dance. If someone invites you to play a game, don't worry about losing, play the game. Don't spend your life watching other people have fun, join in. Even if there are some things you cannot do, or don't have the money, or the time to do, there are other things you can do. Figure out what you like to do and do it.

Baby G: Does that mean I should not watch TV, or watch videos on a computer or phone? What if that is what I like to do?

Summer: The idea is to have balance in your life, do both, watch things you cannot participate in, and participate in things you can. There is room in your life for both.

Willie: I like to watch videos of lady giraffes trying to balance on one leg. I like to have some balance in my life. 😂

Baby G: World, don't just be a spectator, be a participant too. Don't spend your life watching other people have fun, join in. Life is better when you do both, watch and participate.

Baby G: Mama, what is cheating?

Summer: Baby G, you are cheating if you are doing something you shouldn't, just so you will have an unfair advantage, win a competition, get a better grade, or pass a test. If you deceive someone, if you lie to them, you may cheat them out of something like their inheritance, which is money from their parents. If you are not faithful to your mate, you are cheating on them.

Willie: I cannot cheat on your mama. She is a giraffe, and we giraffes have phenomenal eyesight. She sees and knows everything. 😂

Summer: Willie, you should not cheat, even if no one can see you do it, and no one knows you are doing it. Cheating is wrong.

Baby G: How do people cheat to win?

Summer: Some drugs are legal, but you cannot take them before a competition because they enhance your performance. They make you stronger, faster, or help you keep on going. If you take them when they are not allowed, you are doping. That is cheating. Other ways to cheat are: you use equipment that is not allowed; you don't follow the rules; you don't stay on the course; you catch a ride to the finish line, etc. If you win, and later, they discover you cheated, they will disqualify you, and take your medal or ribbon away. They will give it to the person who finished right after you. You may be banned from participating in that sport. You should be ashamed of yourself.

Baby G: How do they cheat on a test?

Summer: If the test is supposed to determine how well you remember something, and you use notes to come up with an answer, that is cheating. If you use someone else's answer, or have them take the test for you, that is cheating too. There is a saying, "Winners never cheat, and cheaters never win".

Willie: That saying is wrong. Obviously if you cheat to win, you are a winner that cheated. Or are you a cheater that won? 😂

Summer: Willie! That saying is not wrong. It means you should not cheat if you want the world to see you as a winner, and not as a cheater. Baby, even if you only cheat once, people will wonder if every time you won in the past, did you cheat? Will you cheat again? You will lose people's trust. There is another saying, "May the best man win".

Willie: That saying is wrong too. What if you are a giraffe, or a woman, or a child? You may be the best and should win! 😂

Summer: Willie, that saying isn't wrong either. It means you hope the person who is the most deserving wins, whether that person is a giraffe or a human, is a male or a female, or is young or old. That person is the most talented, or is the most skilled, or is the hardest working, and they played fair. That person didn't cheat their way to the win.

Baby G: World, cheating, no matter where or how you do it, is wrong. Don't be a cheater. May the best male, female or child, whether a giraffe or human, win!

Baby G: Mama, what does "monkey see, monkey do" mean?

Willie: You see me do something, you do it, and people say what a cute monkey you are. You stop being a giraffe, and start being a monkey. 😂

Summer: Willie, he will never stop being a giraffe, no matter what he does! Baby G, monkeys are primates, in the same family as humans. Monkeys like to mimic, copy, what others do. They don't understand why something is being done. Don't act like a monkey, don't do things without understanding why you are doing them. That saying, "monkey see, monkey do" also means be careful what you do, because others, especially children, will watch, and will mimic you, without understanding why you do it. Parents need to realize they are role models for their kids. Not everything a parent does is good for their children to do.

Baby G: Like what?

Summer: You have been mimicking what your daddy does, bumping your neck on me, trying to block me from leaving the area, etc. You see he does it, so you do it, without understanding why he does it. Monkey see, monkey do.

Willie: Why don't you mimic your mama's hay showers instead and toss me that hay to make up for what she takes. She takes more than her fair share. But to be fair, she shares the showered hay with you. 😂

Summer: Willie! I keep telling you, we all share that common feeder. You have plenty of hay in your private feeder. Besides, nothing is stopping YOU from mimicking my hay showers. Unless, of course, you are willing to admit that you still don't understand why I do them?

Baby G: What else do monkeys do?

Summer: They have long, strong, prehensile tails. Prehensile tails are flexible, they can bend, and grasp things. Monkeys use their tails to grab tree branches, so they can run and jump from branch to branch. They also use their tails to grab and eat food. Many monkeys live in trees.

Willie: They are so close to the trees, their heads are right up against the trees. They cannot see the forest for the trees. 😂

Summer: Willie, that expression, "can't see the forest for the trees" means you are only looking at the details, you need to back away, and look at the whole or big picture. Baby, monkeys are used in other sayings. When you say something is "more fun than a barrel of monkeys", you think it is amusing. There are three wise monkeys who "see no evil, hear no evil, speak no evil". The first one covers his eyes, the second one covers his ears, and the third one covers his mouth.

Baby G: Does anybody else imitate things?

Summer: Apes are also primates. They are usually larger than monkeys, and do not have tails. To ape someone is to imitate them, usually in a mocking way. You make fun of someone or something they do. Don't do that. Parrots are birds. Parrots cannot talk, but they can imitate sounds. To parrot someone is to repeat what they say, without understanding what the words mean. Don't do that either.

Baby G: World, don't mimic, ape, or parrot what you don't understand. Parents, be careful what you do in front of children. They may mimic what you do.

Baby G: Mama, what is a rumor?

Summer: Baby G, a rumor is a story that you hear and tell others. It may not be true. You spread the rumor. Let's play an old game called Telephone. It will help you understand rumors. Pick someone to go first. They whisper something, say something in a low voice, to the person next to them. That person repeats what they think they heard to a third person, and so on. The last person in the group says out loud what they heard.

Baby G: Why is that game fun?

Summer: Often, people don't hear the whispers correctly, so the original message gets distorted or changed. It is a fun game, unless you are deaf, and cannot hear whispers at all. I will whisper something to your daddy.

Willie: Okay, now I will whisper what I think I heard to you. Or maybe I will make up something wild? Can a captive giraffe wear wild makeup? 😂

Summer: Willie, please follow the rules of the game. Try to repeat what you think you heard.

Baby G: I am the last one in the group, right? So, I should say out loud what I think I heard?

Summer: Yes. What did you hear?

Baby G: I am pregnant, I have a baby in my belly!

Summer: You are not pregnant! If you were, you'd be the first male giraffe in history to get pregnant. You know how many people watched your birth. Could you imagine how many would watch THAT birth?! That Telephone game shows how what I said, which was, "I am not pregnant, I have a grain belly", got distorted.

Willie: Yeah, I thought she said, "I am not pregnant, I have no baby in my belly." I wish she said what you said. 😂

Summer: Willie! That is how rumors start. Baby, someone misheard something, and passed along what they thought they heard. Sometimes, they pass along what they wish they heard. Don't spread rumors. Before you pass information on to someone else, check and see if it is true. Verify the information. Look at the source, the person or thing, where the information came from. Decide if the source can be trusted to give you correct and complete information.

Don't leap or jump to a bad conclusion, based on what you think you heard, or what you wanted to hear. Don't make the wrong judgment or decision, based on incorrect or incomplete information.

Willie: Speaking of leaps, does a leap year leap to a bad conclusion? What does it think it heard? 😂

Summer: Willie, years, whether leap years or not, don't leap to conclusions! However, a year or an event can come to a conclusion, it ends. Baby, years that are evenly divisible by 4 are usually leap years. The year 2016 was the last leap year. The year 2020 will be the next leap year. Century years, those that are evenly divisible by 100, are usually not leap years. The year 2100 will not be a leap year. A century year is a leap year if it is also evenly divisible by 400. The year 2000 was a leap year. Today is February 28. This year is not a leap year, since 2018 is not evenly divisible by 4. So, there won't be a February 29 this year. There won't be a leap day. Tomorrow will be March 1.

Baby G: World, don't spread rumors. Before you pass on information, verify it is true, and it came from a source you trust. Don't leap to a bad conclusion, based on what you think you heard, or what you wanted to hear.

Now, don't just see, observe. Are the windows low enough that you can see out?

Baby G: No. They are too high for me to see out. But you and Daddy are tall enough to see out the bottoms of the windows.

Summer: You don't have a window at your height, because you could accidentally break it, and get hurt. So, the tops of the windows are higher than we are tall. I am between 14 and 15 feet tall. What does that tell you about the windows?

Baby G: They are at about 14 or 15 feet off the ground? The tops of the windows are even higher?

Willie: I observe that I deserve a feeder by the windows. I want to eat at a restaurant with a view. 😂

Summer: Willie, you can grab a bite of hay and chew it by your window. Then when you chew your cud, you can enjoy another meal at your "restaurant" with a view. Baby, yes, you didn't just see the windows with us in front of them. You observed we can see out the bottoms of our windows, but you cannot because you are shorter than us. You observed how high the windows are compared to how tall we are. You learned about things around you, not just by seeing them, but by observing them.

Baby G: World, there is plenty to see around you. But don't just see it, observe it! You will learn a lot by observing things.

Baby G: Mama, what is a blindside?

Willie: People who are blind cannot see. That means they cannot see any side of you. If you only look good on your blind side, where the blind people are, you are ugly. I look good on all sides. I have no blind side. 😂

Summer: Willie, that is not what the word 'blindside' means! Baby G, the compound word 'blindside' contains the word 'blind'. Words or phrases containing the word 'blind' mean you can't see something. Look in front of you. Don't move your head. Because you are not blind, you can see very well what is in front of you. You might be able to see what is next to your left side or your right side, but you won't be able to see further back. You cannot see what is directly behind you. You have blind spots where you cannot see. You can use mirrors to eliminate the blind spots. That is why cars have mirrors on their left and right sides, and a rear-view mirror inside the car.

Willie: I would rather use the mirrors on my car to see myself, looking so splendid in my scarf. Maybe that is why I was blindsided, and didn't see what hit me? 😂

Summer: Willie, use those mirrors to see the other cars and the road, not yourself! Baby, a blindside is something you don't see coming. You are hit from behind, or where you are vulnerable. You are led to believe one thing, then something else happens. You think you will get a pleasant surprise, but you get an unpleasant one instead. You are blindsided.

Baby G: Like what?

Summer: Someone promises you a treat for doing something, then afterwards, they tell you they cannot give you the promised treat. They pretend they ran out of treats when they never intended to give you any.

Baby G: They lied?

Summer: They lied to get you to do what they wanted. They don't care that you didn't get what you expected or wanted.

Willie: Don't forget to open your eyes. I forgot once after waking up, and I thought I was blind. Then I remembered to open my eyes, and I started singing, "Amazing Grace ... T'was blind, but now I see ...". Talking about 'hymns', why aren't there any 'herns'? 😂

Summer: Willie! You are mixing up the word 'him' with the word 'hymn'. Do something amazing and let us talk. Baby, hymns are religious songs or poems. If something opens your eyes, it makes you realize or discover what you thought was true is not actually true.

Baby G: Are there other "blind" words or phrases?

Summer: If you turn a blind eye to something, you deliberately ignore it, you pretend you don't see it, or pretend you don't know it is happening, even though you do see it and you know it is wrong. You can be temporarily blinded by too much light, or if you injure your eyes. A saying, "the blind leading the blind", means someone who knows nothing asks someone else for help, and that person also knows nothing. An incompetent person tries to teach someone else who is equally incompetent. Nobody knows what they are doing.

Baby G: World, if you can see, help those who can't. Don't turn a blind eye when you know someone is doing something wrong. Don't blindside anyone.

Baby G: Mama, what is rudeness?

Summer: Baby G, when someone doesn't care about your feelings while doing or saying something to you, they are rude. They are inconsiderate or not polite. They embarrass or offend you or others. They say or do rude things. If you are rude, you look like you have no manners, and as if you weren't taught to behave better than that. People won't tolerate your rudeness.

Willie: I wasn't taught the difference between crude and rude. Can you "c" the difference? 😂

Summer: Willie, crude and rude are similar words, but usually, someone who is rude intends to be rude. Something or someone that is crude is in its or their natural, rough, unrefined state.

Baby G: What are some examples of rudeness?

Summer: If you are saying something that you don't know is wrong, and someone loudly tells everyone else that you are wrong, instead of just letting you know about your mistake, that is rude. If someone yells out, "you are terrible", while watching children practice their roles in a school play, that's rude. Children need to practice before they can be good at anything. People may make rude, unwanted comments about someone's age or weight. Someone may say anyone watching us on the live cam must be "an old, fat, lady who doesn't have a life". That is not true. Many people, the young ones and the old ones, the skinny ones and the fat ones, the males and the females, enjoy both watching us online, and doing other things in real life. Those are overt, obvious, cases of rudeness. Rudeness can be subtle, small, indirect, and not so obvious.

Baby G: What is subtle rudeness?

Summer: Often, the rude person doesn't think they are rude, but they still don't think about how what they do affects others. They make plans that don't include someone right in front of that person.

Willie: That's why your mama doesn't like my plans for the lady giraffes at Cheyenne Mountain Zoo. Because I make them right in front of her, and they don't include your mama. I should not be rude and make those plans when she isn't here to hear them. 😂

Summer: Willie! That isn't why! Don't make such plans whether I am here to hear them or not! Baby, rude people ask someone to wait for them to do something, and then take their sweet time doing it. They don't hurry. They walk up to two people who are talking, and demand to know what they are talking about. They insist on being a part of the conversation which had nothing to do with them, and then they take over the conversation. They change the subject and talk about what they want.

Willie: Did you hear about the naked guy who interrupted a conversation? He was a nude dude who was rude. 😂

Summer: Willie, it is you who is being rude, interrupting us to tell us an inappropriate joke. Let us talk.

Baby G: Is interrupting people always rude?

Summer: No. If there is an emergency, you must interrupt to warn others to get to safety.

Baby G: World, don't be rude. Don't deliberately embarrass or offend anyone. Show you were taught to behave better than that. Be considerate of other people's feelings. Think about how what you do affects them.

Baby G: Mama, what is Women's Day?

Willie: It is the day after a Girls' Night Out. They wake up in the morning with headaches, and realize they are women now, and not girls any longer. They are too old to party that hard. Is Women's Day a day of mourning their lost youth, or is it the morning after a lost night? 😂

Summer: Willie, it is neither. Baby G, today is March 8. It is International Women's Day. It celebrates the achievements of women all over the world. It also seeks equality between men and women.

Baby G: Is it just for humans? Are female giraffes also celebrating?

Summer: It is mainly for humans, but we giraffes can celebrate it too. Both genders, males and females, celebrate International Women's Day, not just the females. Equality between the genders is a good thing, whether you are a human or a giraffe, or you are a male or a female.

Baby G: What is equality?

Summer: Two things can be equal in many ways. If we both have 3 carrots, we have an equal number of carrots. If we both have a large carrot, we have equal sizes of carrots.

Willie: Didn't you read Animal Farm? All giraffes are equal, but some bull giraffes are more equal than others. Give me those carrots! 😂

Summer: Willie! No animal is more equal than others! Baby, equality means men and women, bull giraffes and lady giraffes, have equal status, rights and opportunities.

Baby G: What is equal status?

Summer: Your status is where you rank in a group or organization, at the top, or in the middle or at the bottom. It is also the condition of something at a particular time, or what has been done so far. How you are treated by a doctor depends on how sick you are, your health status. Men and women should have equal status in their homes and their countries.

Baby G: What are equal rights?

Summer: Depending on where you live, you have certain rights, such as the right to believe what you want to believe, the right to live your life as you wish, the right to live where you want, etc. You have these rights so long as you don't hurt others. Men and women living in the same country should have equal rights. It would be great if they had equal rights all over the world.

Baby G: What are equal opportunities?

Summer: An opportunity is a chance to do something, get a better job, live somewhere else, make a change, or do something new. If a boy and a girl are equally ready and able to do something, they both should be given the chance to do it. Men and women should have equal opportunities.

Baby G: Aren't men better at certain things and women at other things?

Summer: Yes, men usually are stronger, women usually have more endurance, etc. But when it comes to things they can do equally well, both should have equal chances, and equal rewards. They should be paid the same, if they are really doing the same work, and not just similar work.

Willie: I can reach higher than a human can, so they should pay me more for licking the wood clean. 😂

Summer: Willie, you lick the wood because it has hay dust and minerals, not for pay! Besides, humans can reach as high as you can if they use a ladder.

Baby G: World, let's celebrate what women have achieved, and seek equality for all, male and female, whether a human or a giraffe. Happy International Women's Day!

Baby G: Mama, what does benign mean?

Willie: Today is March 9. In some places, they write it this way: 9 March. It be nine of March. 😂

Summer: Willie, he asked about the word 'benign'. Anyway, you should say "today is the ninth of March", not "it be nine of March". Baby G, when you count things, like carrots, you can put them in order. You have the first (1st) thing, the second (2nd) thing, the third (3rd) one, the fourth (4th) one, the fifth (5th), the sixth (6th), seventh (7th), eighth (8th), ninth (9th), tenth (10th), eleventh (11th), twelfth (12th), thirteenth (13th), fourteenth (14th), fifteenth (15th), sixteenth (16th), seventeenth (17th), eighteenth (18th), nineteenth (19th) and twentieth (20th). Then you have the twenty-first (21st), twenty-second (22nd), and so on. Next, you have the thirtieth (30th), thirty-first (31st), etc. You do the same for fortieth (40th), fiftieth (50th), sixtieth (60th), seventieth (70th), eightieth (80th), and ninetieth (90th).

Baby G: So, today is the ninth day in the month of March?

Summer: Yes, it is. As for your original question, the word 'benign' means harmless or gentle. Sometimes, people get sick, and have lumps inside or outside of their bodies where they shouldn't be.

Willie: I have lumps inside my stomach. They are lumps of carrots. They are exactly where they should be. They stay there, until I am ready to chew my cud, then they are lumps in my mouth. I love carrot flavored cud. 😂

Summer: Willie! Go chew your cud and let us talk. Baby, when people get lumps, or tumors, where they should not be, sometimes the tumors are harmless, they are benign. Other times they are harmful, they are malignant. They might be cancerous. If they are from cancer, that is very bad. They may spread through the body. Doctors try to fix or get rid of the cancer. Sometimes, they can do that, and the sick person gets well. The cancer is not cured, it just goes away. The cancer goes into remission.

Baby G: How can I make sure I never get cancer?

Summer: You can't. You can reduce the chance, by not eating certain foods, and by trying to avoid certain things believed or known to cause cancer, like smoking, etc. Sometimes, you can have surgery, an operation, and remove part of your body, to try to prevent getting cancer in that part. Sometimes, you have family with cancer, which makes it more likely you will too. There is nothing you can do about that. You can pick your friends, but you cannot pick your family, or your genes. Sometimes, it is just bad luck.

Willie: It is a shame that I cannot pick my family. I'd pick up a bunch of lady giraffes. If I am the only male giraffe in the family, I will have better luck with the females. 😂

Summer: Willie, picking and picking up are not the same thing! Keep pressing your luck, and you will have fewer lady giraffes in your family, not more.

Baby G: What can I do if someone I know has cancer?

Summer: You can support them, and let them know you care, and that they are not alone.

Baby G: World, if you are unlucky enough to get cancer, I hope your doctors can help you, and your cancer will go into remission. I care about you, and hope you know you will never be alone. I am here.

"Daylight Savings"

Tasha Poochette

Baby G: Mama, what is Daylight Savings Time?
Willie: Inside a Savings and Loan, there is a vault. Your money is saved in there. Vaults are dark inside. Money doesn't like being "a loan" in the dark. You could burn the money to light it up. Or you could put daylight between you and your savings. That is Daylight Savings. 😂
Summer: Willie, money doesn't care about being alone in the dark! It is you who is in the dark about what Daylight Savings Time is. Baby G, a Savings and Loan is a type of bank. Your money is saved, or stored, in a bank vault. Money is taken out of the vault and loaned to other people. They borrow the money, and use the loan to buy things, like a new house.
Willie: They used my money to buy themselves a house? Instead, they should use my money to build me a bachelor barn with lots of room for new lady giraffes. 😂
Summer: Willie! You are not a bachelor! If you keep talking like one, you will need your money to get yourself a new bachelor pad. Baby, later, the borrower pays back the loan. They give the bank even more money, called interest, to thank the bank for giving them a loan. The bank pays you interest because you saved your money in their vault. If you are burning money, or putting daylight between you and your money, you are using a lot of money, buying a lot of unnecessary stuff. You are using your money quickly instead of saving it. Daylight Savings Time means clocks and watches are set an hour ahead. In the Spring, they "spring forward". For example, if it is really 9 p.m., they are set to 10 p.m. In the Autumn or Fall, they are set an hour back. They "fall back". If it is really 2 a.m., they are set to 1 a.m.
Baby G: Why do they do that?
Summer: As you know, when the sun is up, it is daylight out. If you set the clock ahead, it will be darker early in the morning, and lighter later in the day. You are "saving daylight" for later in the day, when people are home from school or work. They can do more things outside.
Willie: I want to do more things outside, but there still is snow out there. Is there a Snow Go Away Time? 😂
Summer: Willie, it will soon be springtime, and the snow will go away.
Baby G: Does everybody use Daylight Savings Time?
Summer: It depends on where you live. Tomorrow at 2 a.m., Daylight Savings begins. Most people don't want to get up in the middle of the night to change their clocks, so they will do it tonight before they go to bed. Some clocks automatically make the change.
Baby G: World, try to save some of your money. Try not to burn money. If you live where they have Daylight Savings Time, don't forget to set your clock or watch forward tonight.

Baby G: Mama, what is a catnap?
Willie: A kidnap is where you steal a kid. Therefore, a catnap is where you steal a cat. 😂
Summer: Willie, that isn't what catnap means! Baby G, even though the two words, 'kidnap' and 'catnap', look similar, they mean totally different things. Anyone, not just a kid, can be kidnapped by a bad person. The kidnapper wants a ransom, usually money, in exchange for returning the person who was kidnapped.
Willie: You remember that time you thought I accidentally locked our kid in my pen with me? You didn't know that was deliberate. I kidnapped him and wanted you to ransom him by giving me carrots. 😂
Summer: Willie! Kidnapping is a crime, and eventually, kidnappers will be caught, and go to jail. Baby, a catnap is a brief, or short sleep, usually during the day. You doze off or take a nap. It is usually a light sleep. It is easy to wake up from it.
Baby G: Why is it called a catnap?
Summer: Cats sleep often, and for short times during the day. They can doze for hours, but usually they sleep in the sunlight for only a few minutes at a time. Their total time sleeping each day is 12 to 16 hours. That is a lot of sleep, when you think about it. Each day only has 24 hours in it. They sleep their lives away. In the wild, giraffes sleep only for minutes at a time. Their total time sleeping is 30 minutes or so per day. We captive giraffes are much safer than wild giraffes, so we can sleep for longer stretches at a time, and sleep much longer per day, up to 4 or 5 hours.
Baby G: Is there a giraffenap?
Summer: No. Humans and giraffes take catnaps, or just naps. Humans that are working may take a short power nap in the middle of the work day to refresh themselves. Children in kindergarten may take naps in the middle of the school day. Giraffes sometimes take power naps with one eye open, watching their babies, and keeping an eye out for lions.
Baby G: Does everyone like naps?
Summer: Children often don't like taking naps. They feel like they are missing out on something good while they sleep. Adults often love naps. They feel like naps restore something missing from themselves. Often, adults don't sleep well at night and need naps during the day. Today is National Napping Day. It is the day after Daylight Savings Time begins. People nap to catch up on the sleep they lost when the clocks were moved an hour ahead.
Willie: I nap to get through the hours until my next meal. Meanwhile, I dream about my next meal. 😂
Summer: Willie, don't sleep away your life. But enjoy your naps.
Baby G: World, Happy National Napping Day! I hope you enjoy your naps.

Baby G: Mama, why do you do art?

Summer: Baby G, art is a way to show the world what you see, or what is important to you, what is in your heart.

Baby G: I have art in my heart?

Willie: Of course, you do, everyone does. Don't you see the word 'art' is inside the word 'heart'? 😂

Summer: Willie, that is true, but not what it means when you say what is in your heart. Baby, your heart keeps you alive. It pumps blood to your lungs, through your body, and back again. Your heart is very important. If it doesn't work right, you will get very sick or die.

Willie: Eating a lot of carrots is very important to me. I say what is in my heart. But I wish the carrots were in my stomach, not my heart. 😂

Summer: Willie! Your heart doesn't actually contain carrots! Your heart is both real and symbolic. It is a symbol of what you really want. Baby, when you say what is in your heart, you talk about what is important to you, what you believe. If your heart is hard or bitter, it will show up in what you say. If you really want to do something, you put your heart into it. You find it in your heart to forgive someone who hurt you. You keep your most secret thoughts and deepest beliefs in your heart of hearts. If you are very scared or nervous about something, your heart is in your mouth. If you learn or know something by heart, you have memorized it. If you have a good heart, you are a kind person. If you have a lot of heart, you are a loving, caring person.

Baby G: What is blood for?

Summer: The air you breathe contains oxygen. Your lungs put oxygen in your blood. The blood also contains nutrients from food. Your body has cells. The cells need oxygen and nutrients to live. The cells cooperate to keep you alive and moving. Blood carries oxygen and nutrients to your cells. After the oxygen and nutrients are used, your blood carries away waste, which is removed by your kidneys. The blood returns to your heart, and the cycle begins again.

Willie: What is the point in doing something over and over again? That is boring. 😂

Summer: Willie, the point is to keep you alive, so you can think about what is boring or not. Be glad your body is willing and able to do the same thing over and over again. Even if doing art over and over again was boring, which it isn't, I would still do it.

Baby G: So, art is important to you?

Summer: Yes. But what it does is also important to me. People like buying my art. The money raised by selling off my art helps giraffes in the wild. That is a good cause.

Baby G: Can Daddy and I also do art? I want to help raise money for that cause.

Summer: You need to be trained first. They trained me to hold a paintbrush with paint on it in my mouth and press it against a canvas. They reward me with carrots or lettuce when I do that. They pick the paint colors, but I decide what to paint.

Baby G: World, do art to show what is important to you. Put your heart into it. Buy Mama's art. She does it for a good cause.

Baby G: Mama, what is Pi?

Willie: Pi is a round thing you eat. Or is it something you get around to eating? 😂

Summer: Willie, that is a pie. Baby G, today is Pi Day. 'Pi' with no letter E on the end is a number that begins with 3.14. Today is March 14, or 3/14. In some places, it is written as 3.14. People call it Pi Day. To celebrate, they eat pies, which do have the letter E.

Baby G: What is Pi used for?

Summer: Every circle has a middle, its center. If you draw a line from one side or edge of the circle, through the middle, to the other edge, the line is called the diameter of the circle. The diameter has a length, in inches or feet or yards. In some places, the diameter is measured in centimeters or meters. Now suppose you want to know how big the circle is. If it is a really big circle, you could walk around it, and count your steps. Then you could measure how long each one of your steps is and multiply those two numbers. That would tell you how big the circle is. But what if the circle is too small for you to walk around it? That is where Pi comes in. You measure the diameter of the circle using a ruler, or a measuring tape, or some other device. Then you multiply the diameter by Pi to get the length of the circle, or its circumference. You will know how big it is.

Baby G: I don't understand.

Summer: We have a concrete floor covered with some mats and pine shavings. I will clear off some shavings, so you can see the mat. Then I will push some shavings into a circle on the mat. Do you see the circle?

Baby G: Yes, I see the pine shavings make a circle.

Summer: The diameter of my circle is two feet. I want to multiply the diameter by Pi, which really has many digits in it. To keep this simple, we will just use the first three digits, or 3.14. So, I will multiply the diameter, 2 feet, by 3.14. That equals 6.28 feet. The pine shaving circle is 6.28 feet around, or just over 6 1/4 feet.

Baby G: So, we use Pi to figure out how big a circle is. What is Pie for?

Willie: I just got done multiplying by Pi. I would rather multiply my pies and have many of them. 😂

Summer: Willie, giraffes don't eat pie, but humans love it. I suppose you could make pies out of carrots and lettuce. Baby, humans make pie using different ingredients. Depending on what is in it, it can be the main meal, or a dessert. There are pizza pies, meat and potato (meat and tater) pies, pot pies, shepherd pies, cottage pies, etc. There are fruit pies, cream pies, custard pies, etc. You can make a pretend pie out of mud, wet dirt. Or you can have a "mud pie" made of a cookie (biscuit) crust, coffee ice cream, caramel and whipped cream. The important thing is all pies (except real mud pies) should taste good, and they should be round like a circle. You could share some pie with your circle of friends.

Willie: If you share your pie, there is less for you. Keep your circle of friends small, or better yet, have no friends, then there will be more pie for you. 😂

Summer: Willie, it is better to have less pie, and a bigger circle of friends to share it with. Eating alone can be lonely.

Baby G: World, today is Pi Day. Enjoy a pie while using Pi to figure out how big your circles are. I am glad you are in my circle of friends. I wonder how big that circle is?

Baby G: Mama, what is a baby boom?

Willie: When babies scream, it is so loud, it is like a sonic boom. They are baby booms. 😂

Summer: Willie, giraffe babies can make low sounds that humans can hear, but they lose that ability. Human babies do scream loudly, but that isn't a sonic boom or a baby boom. Baby G, if you drop a pebble, or a little rock, into a puddle of water, it makes waves of water that move away from the rock. Similarly, sounds travel in waves through the air, and into your ears. You hear them. If an airplane or another aircraft moves faster through the air than sound waves do, it is traveling faster than the speed of sound. That causes a sonic boom, a very loud noise. It sounds like an explosion, or like very loud thunder.

Willie: If our baby moves away quickly, will that cause a sonic boom of people crying? Will you be able to hear them sob over my cheers? 😂

Summer: Willie! Our baby is here for the rest of the 2018 season. Nobody, not even you, will cheer if he must leave. But if he does, it will be to have a mate and babies of his own. We all cheer when more captive giraffe babies are born, because wild giraffe populations are dropping so fast. Baby, a baby boom is a big increase in the number of babies born in one place or one country. The population jumped because so many babies were born.

Baby G: Were they all born on the same day?

Summer: Some were, but most were born that year, or in following years. After World War II, the birth rate in the USA jumped so much, people born between 1946 and 1964 were given their own group name: Baby Boomers. There were so many of them, that in the future, there will be more people over the age of 65 in the USA, than under the age of 18.

Baby G: What is a birth rate?

Summer: The birth rate is the total number of babies born alive, per 1000 people or animals, born in a year. It is the number of live births per thousand population per year.

Willie: I keep trying to increase the birth rate around here, but it is hard to do. Lady giraffes can only have one new baby per fifteen months, and there is only one lady giraffe here. 😂

Summer: Willie, there will be no lady giraffes here, if you keep talking about getting more lady giraffes!

Baby G: Are there other groups?

Summer: Yes. Generation X includes those born between 1965 and 1976. Generation Y, or Millennials, includes those born between 1977 and 1994. Generation Z includes those born between 1995 and 2009.

Baby G: I was born in 2017. What generation am I?

Summer: I think your generation has been named Generation Alpha. Plus, you are part of a mini baby boom of captive giraffes born last year, and this year. Today is your 11-month birthday. Happy Birthday Baby G.

Baby G: World, whatever generation you are part of, I hope all your birthdays are happy ones.

Paddy Wagon

Kiss Me, I'm Irish

Tasha Poochette

Baby G: Mama, what is blarney?

Willie: I was talking to my friend Arnie, and I accidentally bit my tongue. That made it hard to talk. I said, "You are a really great guy, a tall giraffe among giraffes, blah, blah, Blah-Arnie. I know you can get me those leaves off that tall acacia tree there." 😂

Summer: Willie, if you accidentally bite your tongue, it hurts and swells. That may make it hard to talk. If you "bite your tongue", that means you are trying really hard not to say something that you really want to say. Baby G, blarney is friendly talk that is meant to charm or persuade someone else into doing what you want. It is talk that is too complimentary, too flattering, talk that says too many nice things about someone, so they will be inclined to do what you want. If you kiss the Blarney Stone in Ireland, it bestows, gives, you the gift of flattery. Ireland is near the United Kingdom.

Baby G: Wait, didn't you say before it is in the United Kingdom?

Summer: No, that is Northern Ireland. It is a different country.

Willie: Yeah, the Northern Irish wanted to play with the English. Each player said, "North, I are of England", or Northern Ireland. The other Irish didn't want to play with the English and took their emerald rocks home to Ireland. 😂

Summer: Willie! It is true that the Northern Ireland country is on the same team, in the same U.K., as the English, but that isn't why it is called Northern Ireland! Besides, that is bad English. They would say, "I am north of England", not "North, I are of England". Baby G, Northern Ireland is physically north of Ireland. Ireland is called the Emerald Isle.

Baby G: What are emeralds?

Summer: They are valuable rocks that are emerald green in color. They are gemstones, like diamonds. Green is the official color of Ireland. Today is March 17. It is St. Patrick's Day. He is the patron saint of Ireland. He is believed to have driven the snakes out of Ireland.

Baby G: What are snakes?

Summer: They are reptiles. They are long and skinny like a rope. Bad snakes can bite you, and hurt you, or make you very sick.

Baby G: Are all snakes bad?

Summer: Not all snakes are bad, but until you can distinguish the dangerous ones from the harmless ones, stay away from all of them. People in Ireland, the USA, and some other places, like to dress up in green clothes, wear shirts that say, "Kiss Me, I am Irish", even if they aren't actually Irish, drink green beer, and have parades on St. Paddy's Day.

Willie: Yeah, it is called that, because if you drink too much green beer, you are taken away in a paddy wagon. 😂

Summer: Willie, it is called St Paddy's Day as an affectionate way to refer to St. Patrick.

Baby G: World, whether you dress in green, drink green beer, or aren't even Irish, it is no blarney, I really hope you have a great St. Paddy's Day!

Baby G: Mama, what is a fake apology?

Summer: Baby G, when you do something wrong, you apologize. You say you are sorry. A fake apology is where you say you are sorry, but you don't mean it.

Willie: I am not sorry for my sorry jokes. I mean that. 😂

Baby G: Why would you make a fake apology?

Summer: The reason often depends on how old you are. A little child may run into you, yell, "Sorry", and keep running. They aren't sorry, they didn't stop running, they may not even look at you, they don't care how you feel. They only said, "Sorry", because they were taught to do that, but they still don't understand the purpose of saying it.

Baby G: What is the purpose?

Summer: You say it to acknowledge you know you did something wrong, to say you care about the person you hurt, you want them to know you want to do better next time, and you actually try to do better. You make a sincere, genuine apology, that comes from real feelings.

Willie: What if I don't care about that person? What is better, a fake apology, or an insincere apology? I am trying to do better apologies. 😂

Summer: Willie! If your apology is insincere, it is better not to apologize at all. Better yet, don't hurt anyone, even if you don't like them. You'll have nothing to apologize for.

Baby G: Why would an older kid say, "Sorry", and not mean it?

Summer: They know what they did, or are planning to do, is wrong, but they did it, or do it, anyway. They don't care about the people they hurt. They don't intend to do any better. They are only sorry that they were caught.

Baby G: What about an adult? Why would they do that?

Summer: Adults sometimes say they are sorry, when they don't mean it, because they know apologizing makes them look like a better person. They don't want to BE a better person, just look like one. Then, other people will like them more, or support them more. Sometimes, adults will say one thing to some people, and say something totally different to others. They are two-faced. What they say, or do, depends on who is watching or listening. If caught doing that, they may say they are sorry, but they don't mean it. They should do or say the right thing, no matter who is watching or listening.

Willie: I will not apologize for making bad jokes, no matter who is listening. But I will beg people to listen. It is the right thing to do. At least, it is the right thing to do for me. 😂

Baby G: World, if you do something wrong, apologize. Say you are sorry and mean it. Don't make fake apologies. Acknowledge you know you did something wrong, tell the person you hurt that you care, tell them you want to do better next time, and actually try to do better. Do or say the right thing, no matter who is watching or listening.

Baby G: Mama, is it spring yet?

Summer: Baby G, yes and no. It is March 20, the official start of spring. However, Mother Nature laughs at calendars. Some places, like where we live, still have a lot of rain, snow, and ice. It still feels like winter here. But soon the snow and ice will go away. Then, we can go outside, and not worry about falling down due to any slippery ice. We still must be careful when it rains, because that could cause the ground to be muddy. We don't want to slide in the mud either.

Willie: Spring has sprung! Too bad it sprung a leak. 😂

Summer: Willie, snow and rain both come from water vapor in the air. Rain occurs when the air is warmer, snow when it is colder. So, if it is raining instead of snowing, that shows it is getting warmer. Baby, spring rain helps plants to grow, and they produce spring flowers. Traditional spring colors are green, pink, purple, yellow, etc. They come from those flowers.

Willie: If a watchmaker loses a watch spring in the spring, does he discover where it fell in the fall? 😂

Summer: Willie! Go look for that lost spring and let us talk. Baby G, the Earth we live on is round like a ball. Around the middle of the ball is an imaginary line called the equator. Above the equator is the Northern Hemisphere. Below the equator is the Southern Hemisphere. When the sun moves across the sky, it can cross the equator. This happens twice a year, in the spring, and in the fall. The days on which it happens are called equinoxes. The vernal equinox is the first day of spring in the Northern Hemisphere. In the Southern Hemisphere, the vernal equinox is the first day of autumn, or fall.

Baby G: Why is it called an equinox?

Summer: The word equinox has the same prefix, equ-, as the word equal. It means two things are the same. On an equinox, the day and the night are the same length. From now on, in the Northern Hemisphere, the days are getting longer, and the nights are getting shorter. The reverse is happening in the Southern Hemisphere.

Willie: I must be past my equinox because I keep getting longer, not shorter. 😂

Summer: Willie, you are getting taller, not longer. Besides, you are a young bull giraffe, not a day. You don't have an equinox. You do have a lot of growing to do.

Baby G: World, spring has sprung! I hope it shows up where you are soon. When the snow goes away, we can go outside, and play!

Baby G: Mama, what does "Rock Your Socks" mean?
Willie: You see how many rocks you can put in your socks, and still be able to move. Rocks are heavy! 😂
Summer: Willie, that isn't what "Rock Your Socks" means! Baby G, the word 'rock' has several meanings. One meaning is a stone. Another meaning is a type of music. "Rock Your Socks" means put on mismatched, odd, colorful, or crazy socks.
Baby G: What are socks?
Summer: The word 'sock' also has several meanings. One meaning is to hit someone or something. It is a hard blow, like a sock on the face, or a sock on the jaw. Don't do that. Humans wear clothing on their feet and legs called socks. Socks come in different lengths, patterns, and colors. There are peds (foot socks), micro crew (below the ankle) socks, anklet (ankle) socks, regular crew (calf) socks, knee high socks, stockings, tights, and leggings. Animals may have lower legs that are white or black colored and look like socks or stockings.
Baby G: Why would a human wear mismatched, odd, colorful, or crazy socks?
Summer: Today is March 21. It is Rock Your Socks Day. It is also World Down Syndrome Day. It celebrates people with Down Syndrome.
Baby G: What is Down Syndrome?
Willie: Some people act differently than you or me. They act like drones. They spin around. Then they get dizzy from spinning and fall down. It is Downed Spin-drone. 😂
Summer: Willie! Don't make fun of people who are different than you. Besides, it is Down Syndrome, not Downed Spin-Drone. Baby, remember, you have cells and genes inside you. Those genes are part of chromosomes. Almost every human has the same number of chromosomes as other humans. Almost every giraffe has the same number as other giraffes. Some people have an extra chromosome that makes them look or act different. They have Down Syndrome. Today, people all over the world celebrate their differences, by rocking their socks.
Willie: I wanted to celebrate differently. I socked rocks instead. But it hurts too much when you do that. So, I will celebrate in the same way as everyone else. 😂
Baby G: World, celebrate our differences by rocking your socks today. It is World Down Syndrome Day. Don't make fun of those who look or act different.

Baby G: Mama, what is a stream?
Willie: You could put some water from a STREAM in a bag, heat the bag of water to make STEAM, the bag will burst its SEAM, then the water will run to the SEA. Can you "se" (see) what I did with those words? Where did the letters I took out go? 😂

Summer: Willie, that was quite clever. The letters you removed from those words didn't go anywhere. You just didn't use them in the other words. Baby G, a stream is a small river. Water flows downstream. The stream has a current. Sometimes, fish swim upstream, against the current. A stream may be called a creek.

Willie: If your boat is made of metal, the creek water may rust it. Your rusty boat may have a hole. Water may fill the boat and sink you and your boat. You'll be down the creek with a paddle. 😂

Summer: Willie! That expression is "up a creek without a paddle". It means you are in trouble, or are in a difficult situation, and have nothing to help you out. The situation is hopeless. Baby, water in a stream flows continuously. It starts at a water source, and flows to somewhere else, maybe a lake, or another stream, or to the sea. It doesn't stop, unless the water source is blocked, or it is so hot out that the stream dries up or goes into the ground. The water sources for rivers and streams need to be protected from contamination, from getting bad stuff in them. Animals and humans get fresh water from rivers and streams. Fish live in rivers and streams and will die if the water is contaminated. Some animals and humans eat the fish and can get sick if the fish are contaminated.

Baby G: Are there other types of streams?

Summer: Yes. Anything that continuously flows is a stream. It doesn't stop and start. When you want to watch a video online, you can download it first to your computer or phone, then watch it. Or if you prefer, your computer or phone can continuously receive a video stream from the Internet, as you watch an earlier part of the video. You are streaming the video. You can also stream music to a music player or a phone.

Willie: If you stream a video of a water stream, does the water go by twice as fast? 😂

Summer: Today is March 22. It is World Water Day. The world needs to protect the sources of fresh water, such as rivers and streams.

Baby G: World, Happy World Water Day. Protect the sources of fresh water. We all need fresh water to drink. Without fresh water, we'd be up a creek without a paddle.

Baby G: Mama, what is patience?
Willie: The doctor was impatient, because his patients weren't patiently waiting their turns to be his patients. 😂
Summer: Willie, stop trying my patience, and let us talk. Baby G, if you have patience, you accept it when things aren't going your way, without getting upset. You tolerate trouble, or delay, or pain, or bad luck, without getting angry. You stay calm. You don't complain, or whine. You are patient. The opposite of patience is impatience. You aren't willing to wait for someone or something. You get irritated, when things don't immediately go the way you want. You are impatient. Patience is a virtue.
Baby G: What is a virtue?
Summer: If you behave well, if you are morally good, if you show you have high moral standards, you are virtuous. Some virtues are prudence, justice, fortitude, temperance, faith, hope, and charity.
Baby G: What are those?
Summer: If you are prudent, you are cautious or careful. If you are just, you are unbiased and fair. If you have fortitude, you have courage, you are brave, when you are in pain, or you are in a bad situation. If you have temperance, you don't drink, or eat, a lot of anything that makes you lose control of yourself. You already know what faith, hope, and charity are. There are other virtues. The important thing is you should think about, and do, what is morally right. You should try not to do anything wrong.
Baby G: What are patients?
Willie: Inventors get patents for their inventions. They want the world to know, "I invented that". So, they put the letter I in the middle of the word 'patent'. Patients are inventors with patents. 😂

Summer: Willie! Patients are not inventors with patents! Baby, when a doctor takes care of you, you are his patient. I hope you're seldom a patient, but you are always patient. This is the Serenity Prayer: God, grant me the Serenity to accept the things I cannot change; Courage to change the things I can; And the Wisdom to know the difference.

Baby G: What is serenity?

Summer: When you are serene, you are calm and peaceful. You patiently wait. Currently, the live cam is repeatedly stopping and starting. Sometimes, it stops for hours. The world cannot watch us, and it is getting discouraged.

Willie: You mean the world cannot hear my jokes? I better save them for when they can. 😂

Summer: Willie, they never hear your jokes. Humans cannot hear giraffes hum. It is too low a frequency for them to hear. Remember, a nice lady writes down our conversations, and shares them with the world. The world READS your jokes. Baby, the problem isn't actually the live cam, but the Internet signal to the cam. The problem is being worked. The watchers need to stay calm and be patient. The live cam signal will eventually be fixed. Complaining about it doesn't fix it any faster. Don't send emails about it. Our park owner knows about it and is doing what he can. He is patiently waiting for others to fix what they can, too.

Baby G: World, be patient. The live cam signal will be fixed, and you will be able to watch us again. In the meantime, read the Serenity Prayer. I hope it helps you.

Baby G: Mama, what do colors mean?

Willie: The lady had jaundice, which made the whites of her eyes look yellow. She was so embarrassed, she was red-faced. She held her breath, until she turned blue. She was so sick, her face turned green. She was purple with rage, because no one offered to help her clean up the mess. She was a rainbow. 😂

Summer: Willie, she wasn't a rainbow! Baby G, a rainbow shows up after it rains. It is an arc, a part of a circle, that includes many colors. Some people believe a rainbow is a promise from God, that all rains will end, and God will love all living creatures forever. The meaning of colors depends on what you are looking at. If you see a red rock, it is probably just a red rock. If you see a red gemstone, it may be a ruby, which is more valuable than a diamond. If you see a red ribbon, ask yourself what kind of ribbon is it, and where is it? If it is in someone's hair, it is probably just a pretty hair ribbon. If it is a ribbon you get after a race or a competition, it represents second place. The winner gets a blue ribbon, the second-place finisher gets a red ribbon, and the third-place finisher gets a white ribbon.

Willie: On Independence Day, I wore a red, white and blue ribbon. That is because in the race for independence from England, Americans took first, second, AND third place. 😂

Summer: Willie, that is not why those ribbons have all three colors! The colors come from our flag, which has red and white stripes, and white stars on a blue field. Baby, if someone is wearing a loop of red ribbon, it represents awareness of a disease. They want you to know they support the victims of that disease, and they want to raise money to help fight the disease. Maybe after a lot of time, effort, and money, someone will come up with a cure, and get rid of that disease. If you see a red shirt, sometimes it is just a red shirt. Depending on what day the shirt is worn, or where, or if the wearer is at some special event, the red shirt means different things. It may be part of a uniform, worn by employees at work, or by a soldier. It may represent awareness of a different disease. Different colors of rocks, ribbons, clothes, and many other things, have different meanings.

Baby G: What does purple mean today?

Summer: Today is March 26. It is Purple Day. People want to raise awareness of a disease called epilepsy.

Baby G: What is that? What can we do to help?

Willie: You shake someone who is shaking to make them stop shaking. Or is it you seize her to stop seize-hers? 😂

Summer: Willie! Never make fun of anyone who has a disease! They cannot help what they do. It is not their fault they got that disease. And that word is seizure, not seize-her. Baby, people with epilepsy have epileptic fits, or seizures. They jerk, shake, or make uncontrollable moves. If you don't know what to do when someone has a seizure, go get help from someone who does know. You don't want to make things worse, by "helping" anyone having an epileptic fit, when you have no idea what to do.

Baby G: World, colors can have special meanings. Today's color is purple. Be aware of a disease called epilepsy. Make sure you know what to do if someone has a seizure or go find someone who does know what to do.

Baby G: Mama, what is a mishmash?

Summer: Baby G, a mishmash is an assortment of unrelated things, a hodgepodge. It is a confused mixture. It can also refer to certain foods. Today is Tuesday, March 27. It is a mishmash of things. It is the 86th day of the year, it is Holy Tuesday, it is American Diabetes Association Alert Day, National Joe Day, World Theatre Day, etc.

Willie: Let's 86 this Q&A session and eat. I want to get fat on Fat Tuesday, and not feel hole-y on Holey-Tuesday. Give me some carrots, along with a cuppa Joe, but hold the sugar. I don't want to get an alert that I am at risk of becoming a diabetic. Let's eat, while watching the world debate whether that word is spelled 'theater' or 'theatre'. 😂

Summer: Willie, that was quite a mishmash of ideas in one joke! Baby G, if you 86 something, you throw it away, you get rid of it, you don't want to keep it. A restaurant doesn't offer an eighty-sixed food item anymore, it is off the menu. If you 86 someone, you refuse to serve them.

Willie: I want to 86 any carrot servants that refuse to serve ME. 😂

Summer: Willie! Remember, those people aren't really our servants. They give us carrots because they love us, and they know we love carrots. They want us to be happy.

Baby G: What is a Q&A session?

Summer: A Q&A session is a question and answer session. The Q comes from the word 'question' and the A comes from the word 'answer'. You ask me questions, and I answer them.

Baby G: What are Fat Tuesday and Holy Tuesday?

Summer: Christians celebrate Easter. Lent is the period of 46 days before Easter. It is only 40 days if you omit Sundays. Lent begins on Ash Wednesday. This year, Ash

Wednesday was February 14. Fat Tuesday, or Mardi Gras, is a celebration, a party, that occurs on the Tuesday before Ash Wednesday. Holy Tuesday is the last Tuesday before Easter. It is part of Holy Week. During Lent, some Christians, not all, make a sacrifice, they give up something. They may give up eating meat on Ash Wednesday and on Fridays during Lent. They may give up eating some other favorite food for the whole Lenten season, or they may stop doing something they like doing.

Baby G: What is diabetes?

Summer: Diabetes is a disease. If you are diabetic, your body cannot handle it right when you eat pure sugar, or foods high in sugar, like soda or candy. You end up with too much sugar in your blood. Giraffes don't eat pure sugar, but there is sugar inside carrots. It doesn't have a big impact on blood sugar. You'd have to eat three pounds of carrots to get the same amount of sugar as in one bottle of soda.

Willie: I volunteer to eat those three pounds of carrots if anyone doesn't like carrots. 😂

Summer: Willie, leave us some carrots! Baby, Joe is a name. It is short for Joseph. It also refers to a drink, called coffee. Humans drink coffee or tea alone, or while eating meals. It is best not to watch things on TV or your phone or your tablet while eating. Spend mealtimes talking with your family. Start your own debates. It is fun to debate stuff. By the way, Willie, that word is spelled both ways, 'theater' and 'theatre'. How you spell it depends on where you live.

Baby G: World, today is a mishmash kind of day. Pick what you want to celebrate, or use today to raise awareness about something, or debate something. It is fun!

Baby G: Mama, what are bears?

Willie: Bares are humans who wake up in the spring, and are so sleepy after their long winter's nap, they forget to put any clothes on. Their bare skin gets goosebumps from the cold, and they run around like spring chickens. 😂

Summer: Willie, I cannot bear your bare joke. Go think of another joke and let us talk. Baby G, a human that isn't wearing clothes is nude or naked. If their bare, uncovered, skin gets chilled, little goosebumps may appear. They go away after the human warms up. A spring chicken is a young bird. There is a saying, "you are no spring chicken". It means you are old. Bears are animals that have a lot of fur. They have bear skins but are never bare. There are eight species of bears: North American black bear, brown bear, polar bear, Asiatic black bear, Andean spectacled bear, panda bear, sloth bear, and sun bear. Brown bears aren't always brown in color. Some brown bears are called grizzlies. Some types of bears hibernate in the winter. If you hibernate, you sleep, or you remain inactive (you don't move), or you stay indoors, for a long time. The bears eat a lot of food, then sleep away the winter. They wake up in the spring after their long winter's nap. They are very hungry and mean. Stay away from bears if you can. They can hurt or kill you.

Baby G: What should I do if I meet a bear?

Summer: If the bear notices you, and is paying attention to you, stop, talk in a low, calm voice, and make yourself look as big as possible.

Willie: We giraffes always hum in a low frequency voice, so low that humans and bears can't hear us. I am already as big as possible. Standing tall is what giraffes do. This advice is useless. 😂

Summer: Willie, some of my advice doesn't apply to you. It is not all about you. Learn how things can affect others differently than they affect you, and what they can do. Baby, humans can make themselves look bigger, by putting their arms out or up, and by standing tall. They can stand on a hill to look taller. They cannot outrun a bear. You are a giraffe, and you can outrun a bear. So, my advice to you is: Run. My advice to humans is: Don't run. Bears will chase you if you run. If the bear is not moving, back away slowly, or move sideways, so you won't trip, while keeping your eye on the bear. Then walk away.

Baby G: Anything else I should know?

Summer: Most bears just want to be left alone. But if you mess with her cubs, baby bears, that will make the mama bear very angry. You don't want to mess with an angry mama bear or learn what makes a bear grumpy.

Baby G: Are there any nice bears?

Summer: Yes. Koala bears are cute and cuddly. They actually aren't bears. They are marsupials. But they are still wild animals. Leave them alone. The only safe bear is a toy stuffed bear, called a teddy bear. They were named after Theodore Roosevelt, who had nickname Teddy. He was an American President.

Willie: I am cute and cuddly too. But leave me alone. I don't like being touched. "Don't make me angry. You wouldn't like me when I'm angry". 😂

Baby G: World, enjoy spring, but stay away from bears. Those that just woke up from hibernation are hungry and mean. The rest aren't nice either, unless they are teddy bears.

"Knick-Knack, Paddy-Whack, ——— Give a dog A bone"

Tasha Poochette

Baby G: Mama, what is a children's song?
Willie: Obviously, a children's song is a song sung by children, usually out of tune. I can't wait until you grow up and stop asking dumb questions. Meanwhile, I will tune you out. 😂
Summer: Willie, be nice. He'll grow up soon enough. But I hope he'll always want to learn, and he knows he can always ask me questions, no matter how old he is. Baby G, usually a children's song teaches kids something, like how to count, or how to rhyme, or how to sing in tune. A children's song may have fewer, or easier, words than a regular song.
Willie: I like songs with no words. I don't like idiots who try to talk to me while I am listening. I tell them to shut up. They are so stupid. Don't they know the song should have no words, not even their words? 😂
Summer: Willie! If you insult people, or if you call them names, they are not likely to do what you want. Ask politely, and they will let you listen, without interruptions. Baby, a song with no words is just music. A song puts lyrics, words, with music, or is meant to be sung. If an animal, like a bird, makes music, that is also a song, even though there are no words.
Baby G: Can you teach me a children's song?
Summer: There is a children's song, This Old Man:

This old man, he played one,
He played knick-knack on my thumb,
With a knick-knack, paddy-whack,
Give a dog a bone,
This old man came rolling home.

This old man, he played two,

He played knick-knack on my shoe,
With a knick-knack, paddy-whack,
Give a dog a bone,
This old man came rolling home.

There are more verses, but you get the idea. You can search online for the rest of the lyrics.
Baby G: What is a knick-knack?
Summer: It is a trinket, something you collect and display in your home, like a little statue of a giraffe. Some of our fans have knick-knacks they named after you and me.
Baby G: What is a paddy-whack?
Willie: Your mama's bottom is padded. I give it a whack with my neck. That is a paddy whack. 😂
Summer: Willie, that isn't a paddy-whack! It used to mean hitting an Irishman, but that isn't nice. Now it means to give a spanking to a misbehaving child.
Baby G: Why do dogs get a bone?
Summer: Dogs like to gnaw, chew, on bones. They like to eat meat off the bone, and eat bone marrow, which is inside the bone.
Baby G: Giraffes don't eat meat. Do giraffes chew on bones?
Summer: Yes, but it doesn't happen often. We do it to get a mineral called calcium.
Baby G: World, let's learn some children's songs. They teach kids things like how to count, or how to rhyme, or how to sing in tune. What do you want to sing?

Baby G: Mama, what does 'over' mean?

Willie: I am so over this conversation, even though it just got started. I want to get it over with. 😂

Summer: Willie, go over there, and you won't have to overhear us. Baby G, when something is over something else, it is higher. There is a roof over our barn. We have a roof over our heads. It keeps the rain and snow out. When you go over something, you move on top of it to the other side, or you read it carefully, or you talk about it. You can look over something, like a newspaper. You read parts of it or examine it quickly. We walk over the doorsill to get to the outside. When something is over, it is done, it is finished. When you don't like doing something, or you are afraid of something being done to you, you want to get it over with quickly.

Willie: Pass over those carrots to me. Don't pass over me. I don't want to share. I want to make sure there are none left over for you. I want to eat all of them, and make sure there are no leftovers. But if there are leftovers, they are all for me. 😂

Summer: Willie! You need to learn to share! Sharing food with family and friends, and talking to them at mealtimes, are some of the best experiences in life. Baby, if you pass over food to me, you give it to me. If you pass over someone, you skip them, you ignore them, you don't give them something that everyone else gets. Today is the first day of the Jewish Passover. The Jews celebrate their ancestors who were passed over, spared, when God killed the firstborn of man and beast long ago in Egypt. God freed the ancient Jews from slavery. If there is nothing left over for you, you didn't get what everyone else got.

Leftovers are foods that aren't eaten right away. Leftovers must be eaten in a few days, or frozen, or thrown out.

Baby G: Are there other phrases containing the word 'over'?

Summer: Sure. There are many of them. You do some things over and over again. You repeatedly do them. You lay down several times a day, and you do that every day. But yesterday was different. You laid down, and promptly fell over. You rolled over. You went head over heels. You did a somersault.

Willie: He thought he was doing a lay-over. He laid down, then over he went. 😂

Summer: Willie, a layover is a short period of waiting or rest between two trips, or between two airline flights. Baby, a somersault is a gymnastics trick. It was scary to the world, and to me, when you did that. You need to be more careful when you lay down. Your center of gravity needs to be further back, so you won't fall forward. You won't somersault.

Baby G: Humans can do gymnastics, so why can't I?

Summer: Giraffes cannot safely do somersaults, or other gymnastics. We are not built for that. Some humans are. But they practice, so they can do it safely.

Baby G: World, today is the beginning of Passover. Happy Passover to the Jewish people. If you celebrate, share the food, make sure everyone gets their share, and no one is passed over. If you do gymnastics, make sure you do it safely. You don't want to scare us.

Baby G: Mama, is it foolish to believe something?

Summer: Baby G, it is only foolish to believe something, if someone else can prove what you believe is wrong, it is not true. What belief are you thinking of?

Baby G: I believe there is life after death.

Willie: Don't be a fool. You got that backwards. Everyone knows that you are born, you live, and THEN you die. Death comes after life, not life after death. 😂

Summer: Willie! He is not foolish for believing that! Baby, people who believe in life after death, like us, are not fools. No one can prove our beliefs are wrong. We are not saying you die before you ever lived. We are saying after you live, death is not the end of you. You get to live again in heaven. Today is April 1. It is Easter Sunday. Christians believe Jesus Christ died and rose again. He is risen. They believe in his resurrection and promise. He promised those who believe in him will get to live again in heaven. He said, "I am the resurrection and the life. He who believes in Me, though he may die, he shall live." On Easter, many people go to church, or to a sunrise service. Many, even those who don't believe, like to hunt for Easter eggs, brought by the Easter Bunny. They enjoy Easter baskets, filled with candy, and little gifts. They may wear Easter bonnets, hats, or wear special Easter clothes. Today is also April Fool's Day. It is always on April 1, whereas Easter may be on different days each year.

Baby G: We celebrate fools today?

Summer: Not really. We celebrate bad jokes and pranks played on other people. We play a practical joke, or trick, on them. We want to mislead them, to make them look foolish, or to embarrass them. We don't hurt them, we try to make them laugh at themselves, for falling for the pranks.

Willie: I joke practically every day, but I reserve my practical jokes for April Fool's Day. 😂

Summer: Willie, your jokes are verbal jokes. You tell us the jokes. Baby, a practical joke is more than words. It is physical. You take some action to trick someone. For example, you could put a sign on someone's back, where they cannot see it, telling everyone else to kick that person. The sign says, "Kick me".

Baby G: That isn't nice.

Willie: That doesn't work anyway. We giraffes have long necks and can read signs placed on our backs. 😂

Summer: Willie, that is true. That practical joke is for humans. They cannot see their own backs without using a mirror. Baby, the humans don't kick anyone hard. They just pretend to kick the person wearing the sign, until it dawns on that person what is going on.

Baby G: World, today is both Easter Sunday, and April Fool's Day. Happy Easter to those that celebrate it. Don't call anyone a fool for believing what they do, unless you can prove they are wrong, that what they believe is not true. The only fools today are those who fall for pranks. But keep the pranks funny, and don't harm anyone.

Baby G: Mama, why do things change?

Willie: That one is easy. You make them change. Give me a dollar bill, and I will make change. I will give you two quarters, two dimes, one nickel, and twenty pennies. That is a whole lot of change! 😂

Summer: Willie, don't cheat him. That only is 95 cents. You will owe him a nickel. Baby G, today is the anniversary of the U.S. Mint. Money used in the USA to buy or sell stuff, or to pay someone for their work, is created there. They make paper bills and metal coins. Coins that were not circulated, never used, are called proofs. People collect, or keep, coin proof sets, instead of spending them.

Willie: You don't have proof I spent the coins in your proof set because I spent the proof. 😂

Summer: Willie! Don't steal money in any form! Besides, the coins in proof sets are in mint condition. They should be collected, not spent. They are worth much more than their face value. In other words, a mint quarter is worth much more than twenty-five cents. Baby, some people collect regular coins that were circulated, used. They look for old coins, unusual ones, ones with flaws, or coins from all over the world. Coin collecting is fun. Coin collectors are also known as numismatists. Originally, the U.S. coins were made of gold or silver. Today they are made of regular metals. Keep your eyes open for coins made in 1964 or earlier. They still had silver in them. I believe you were asking about a different kind of change. Things change, become different, for a variety of reasons. As you grow older, your body changes. You get taller, heavier, more skilled at sports, etc. You can do more. What you need to know, what you already know, and what you want to know, all change. These are all good changes. There are bad changes too. You may have to move, leave your friends, change schools, lose a job, etc.

Baby G: What can I do to stop the changes I don't want?

Summer: Sometimes, you can't. You can't control everything that happens to you. Maybe an adult, like a parent or a teacher, can control what happens to you. Sometimes, they can't either. Some changes can't be stopped. But you can control what you do about a change, or how you react to it. If a change can be stopped by someone else, you could talk to them, tell them why you think the change is a bad idea, and suggest different changes that you would like better. You could accept the change and make the best of it. There is a saying, "When life gives you lemons, make lemonade". Lemons are sour fruit. They usually don't taste good. But if you add sugar and water to the juice of lemons, and put the mixture in a tall glass, you get lemonade, a wonderful drink.

Willie: I am like a glass of lemonade. I am tall and sour, not short and sweet. 😂

Baby G: World, you can't control everything that happens to you. You can control what you do about a change, or how you react to it. Some changes are good. Some are bad. Learn which ones are which, and which changes can be stopped. Make the best of changes you cannot stop.

Baby G: Mama, does everyone see things the same way?
Willie: I want you to see things my way, do what I want. It is better that way, at least for me. Can't you see that? 😂
Summer: Willie, see your way out, and let us talk. Baby G, when you see something, light enters your eye, and lands on your retina, which sends signals to your brain via your optic nerve. Then your brain figures out what you are looking at. Your brain is the part of your body that thinks, that understands, that remembers, that controls the rest of your body. Your brain tells your body to move, lay down, stand up, etc. The way everyone sees is the same, but what they see may be different because they have different brains. Look at our blue enrichment bucket. What do you see?
Willie: I see your bucket is full, and mine is empty. How can that be? They must have forgotten to fill mine. I demand food service! They can forget about getting a tip from me. 😂
Summer: Willie! Here is a tip for you: Don't assume they forgot to fill your bucket. Your bucket is empty, because you already ate all of the food that was in it.
Baby G: I see a blue bucket with holes, and there is food in it. We can use the holes to reach the food inside the bucket.
Summer: Yes. That is how most people see it. You saw the bucket has holes, you figured out what the holes are for, and you told me about what you saw. Some people focus on the holes, and not the food in the bucket. They may see holes with blue around them. They may not understand what the holes are for. Their brains may perceive things differently than yours and mine. They focus too hard on something, the holes, that your brain tells you is a small detail. You are comfortable sharing things, or talking about things, with your parents or friends. Some people have a

hard time talking about things. They may not be able to tell others what they see, or how what they see is different from what most other people see. They may not want to tell you. Some people get stuck thinking about something. They cannot think about anything else. Or they do something over and over again. People who focus too much on the small details, who cannot or don't want to tell others what they see, or who think about, or do, things over and over again, may have autism. Today is April 3. April is National Autism Awareness Month. Yesterday was World Autism Awareness Day.

Willie: So, I was supposed to spend yesterday thinking about how people see things, or think, differently than me? I don't think they did a good job of raising my awareness. 😂

Summer: Willie, you should think about stuff like that all year. But think extra hard about it on a special day, or during a specific month. We want the world to be aware of and support people who have autism.

Baby G: World, I wasn't aware yesterday was World Autism Awareness Day. But luckily, I have the whole month of April to raise awareness. Be aware there are people who don't see the world the same way you do, and they might not be able or want to tell you what they do see.

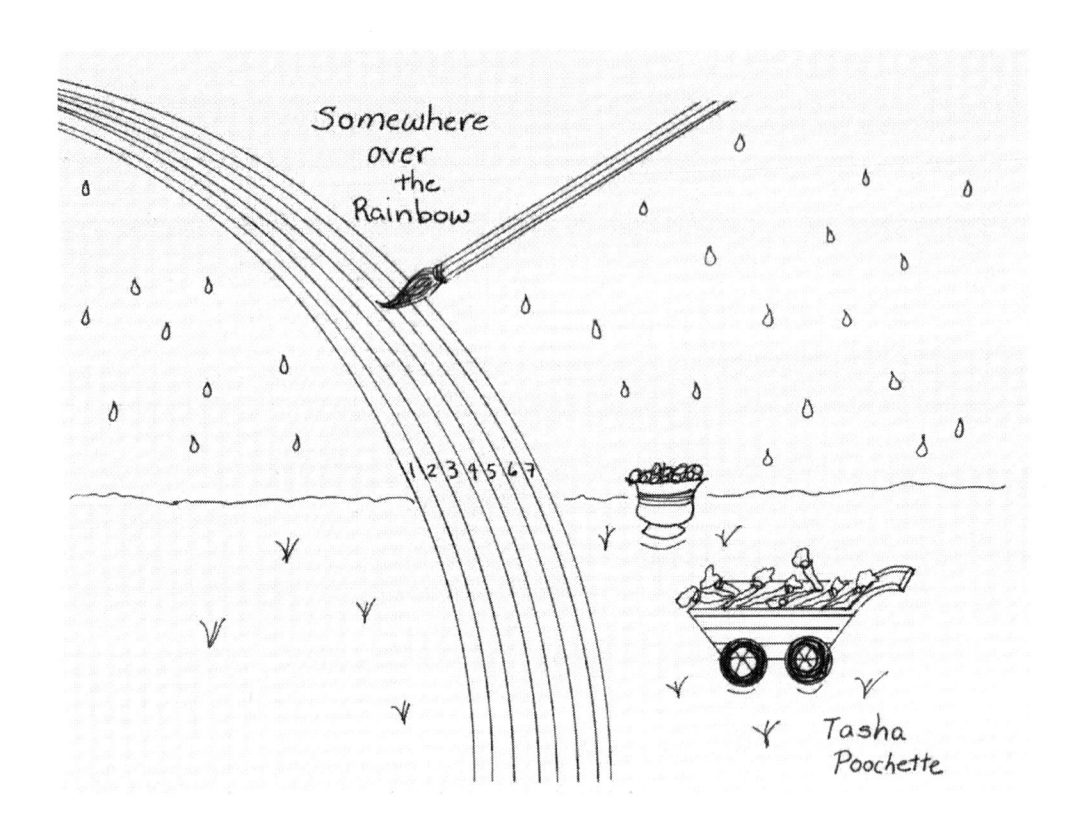

Baby G: Mama, why does a rainbow have seven colors, and not just one?

Willie: Originally, it had one color. God created it and was using a Paint By Numbers set to paint it. He said "One", and it was done. Then He said, "One color is boring. Let's paint it seven colors." After the seventh color, He rested. 😂

Summer: Willie, that is not how the rainbow ended up with seven colors! Baby G, let's figure out why the rainbow has seven colors, and not just one. Light from the sun goes through the sky, through our windows, and along with the overhead barn lights, lights up our door. The door is white. Why isn't the door yellow, like the sun, or blue, like the sky?

Baby G: I don't know. Why?

Willie: Actually, your door has yellowed with age. I do my part to whitewash it with my tongue. 😂

Summer: Willie! Whitewash means you try to make something sound better than it is. You gloss over it or cover up its flaws. Whitewash is also a mixture of lime and water, used to paint a wall white. You lick our door, not to wash it, or to paint it, but to get the minerals and hay dust from it. Baby, the white light from the sun has all colors in it, not just yellow. As the sunlight enters the atmosphere above the Earth, some of the light is bent by molecules in the air. The light is split into its underlying colors, which are scattered. You see the scattered blue light in the sky. Depending on which pigments things have, they absorb, keep, some of the colors, and reflect the other colors. You see those reflected colors. All of the colors in white light are reflected by our door, so it appears as a white door. The mats under our pine shavings absorb all colors, so they look black. Now, let's talk about the rainbow. When the rain falls, the sun may come out from behind the clouds. When white sunlight hits the water droplets still in the air, it is split into the seven colors of the rainbow. A glass prism does the same thing. If you hold it near a wall, and shine a light through it, the prism causes a rainbow to appear on a wall.

Willie: I want a carrot prism. You hold it up to the light, and it causes a wheelbarrow full of orange and yellow carrots to appear. 😂

Summer: Willie, somewhere over the rainbow, an Irish leprechaun may have hidden his pot of gold. Your wheelbarrow full of carrots may be there. Baby, a rainbow has a spectrum of seven colors. A spectrum is a range of things between two ends, or two extremes. People on the autism spectrum have different aspects of it. Some are high functioning. Some are low functioning. But no matter where someone falls on that spectrum, they are important to their family.

Baby G: World, a rainbow isn't just pretty. It is interesting to know why it has seven colors. But no matter what your favorite color is, it is important to know all colors play an equal part in making a rainbow beautiful. The same is true for children with autism. Children with autism, and their brothers and sisters, play an equal part in making their families beautiful.

Baby G: Mama, what is time travel?

Summer: Baby G, time travel is the ability to use a machine to go backwards or forwards in time. You could visit the past before you were born or visit the future after your children are born. You could relive your own history or see your parents when they were young. However, time travel is not real.

Willie: It is not real yet. Maybe someone from the future will invent a time machine, then use it to visit us, then tell me how to invent it. If I invent it first, based on his knowledge, who will get the patent? 😂

Summer: Willie, it would still be his invention. Don't steal other people's ideas. Baby, it is fun to pretend time travel is real, or will become possible. If time travel becomes possible, what time would you like to visit?

Baby G: I would like to visit the time just before I was born, when the world was waiting with you and Daddy, for me to show up. I want to see what they saw and know what they thought about it.

Summer: You don't need a time machine to do that. There are many archived videos of the live cam. Some people took screenshots. Some of those include snippets of the live chat. As your first yearly birthday approaches, people are sharing what they saw, or thought, during my pregnancy and your birth.

Willie: I would use a time machine to go back to yesterday. It was April 4, International Carrot Day. Some guy has the world record for the biggest carrot. I would eat that carrot, then keep using that machine to revisit that day, and eat that carrot over and over again. I would grind that carrot with my teeth. They could make a movie about it, call it Ground Carrot Day. 😂

Summer: Willie! Even though time travel is not real, it has some rules. I am pretty sure you cannot use a time machine to visit the same time over and over. In any case, if you kept eating that carrot over and over again, you would gain so much weight, you would be too big to fit in the time machine! Baby, I'd like to visit the future, where the people who have joined you on your journey, and learned about what they can do, will have saved the giraffes in the wild. I would also like to see our descendants, your children and grandchildren, thrive in captivity. Maybe someday, they could be released into the wild. Remember, we cannot live in the wild. We are captive giraffes that don't know how to survive there, even if there are no bad humans around.

Willie: Giraffes take fifteen months to make babies. That is too long to wait. Summer, we could start making a new baby now, use the time machine to skip those fifteen months, have the new one, start making yet another new one, use the machine again, and … 😂

Summer: Willie, that isn't just against the rules, I would never do that! Part of the joy of having a new baby is waiting for them to arrive and dreaming about what they will be.

Baby G: World, time travel is not real…yet. But it is fun to pretend it is possible. What time would you like to visit?

Baby G: Mama, what does "for better, for worse" mean?

Summer: Baby G, that is a part of a wedding vow. You pledge to stay with your mate, be a team, during good times, when everything is going well, and in bad times, when disasters hit.

Willie: Summer, I pledge to stay with you, my mate, while your food dish is full. Eating together, as a team, is a good time. But when your food dish is empty, that is a disaster. I pledge to split. 😂

Summer: Willie, if you cannot be with me through both good times AND bad times, I have no time for you! Baby, when a human finds a mate, they may get married. They have a wedding ceremony, where they pledge to love one another, and be faithful to each other. A wedding vow is something like: "I, ____, take you, ____, to be my lawfully wedded (husband/wife), to have and to hold, from this day forward, for better, for worse, for richer, for poorer, in sickness and in health, until death do us part."

Baby G: Do giraffes have wedding vows?

Willie: We have our own vows: "I, ____, take you, ____, to be my mate, to have my children, from this day forward, for better, or until someone better comes along, then we part." 😂

Summer: Willie! That is not a giraffe vow! Although it does reflect what bull giraffes, and some humans, want. Baby, giraffes don't get married. Male humans should want to provide for their children and protect them. The best way to do that is to love and be faithful to their child's mother. Not every father marries the mother of their child, but marriage is still the best way to start and be a family. When parents try to stay together, when they try to mate for life, that makes their children happy, it makes them feel secure.

Not every marriage works out. But it is worth trying. Giraffes usually don't mate for life. In the wild, lady giraffes, and their young children, form a tower, and an older bull giraffe may join the tower from time to time. The lady giraffes are faithful to him so long as he stays with them, which may be for life or not. Captive giraffes try to be faithful to their mates, but sometimes humans give them new mates, to help them have more babies. Every new giraffe baby helps save giraffes from going extinct.

Baby G: Do any other animals mate for life?

Summer: Yes. Sun conures, swans, black vultures, albatrosses, turtle doves, and bald eagles, all of which are birds, mate for life. So do gibbons, which are primates like humans, French Angelfish, wolves, termites, which are bugs, prairie voles, which are rodents, and a worm.

Willie: A weak or despicable human is called a worm. If the worm that mates for life is not faithful to his mate, does she call him a human? 😂

Baby G: World, whether you get married or not, whether you mate for life or not, pledge to love one another, and be faithful to each other. Be with your mate for better, for worse, and not just until someone better comes along.

Baby G: Mama, what does unique mean?

Summer: Baby G, the prefix uni- means one. Unique means one of a kind. Something that is unique is not like anything else. A unicorn is unique.

Willie: I am unique too. I am one of a kind, a giraffe comedian. No one else is like me, but I hope everyone likes me. 😂

Summer: Willie, we all like you, but I would like you more, if you'd let us talk.

Baby G: What does a unicorn look like?

Summer: Since it is a mythical creature, no one has actually seen one. But most people think it is a white horse, with one pointed, straight or spiraling horn on its forehead. It has a flowing mane and long tail. It is a symbol of purity, innocence, and magic. It is the national animal of Scotland. Today is April 9. It is National Unicorn Day. It is celebrated in the USA and the UK.

Willie: We need more days that celebrate giraffes. If a giraffe has one ossicone, would it be a uni-cone? 😂

Summer: Willie, go look for one. If you find it, then we will celebrate National Uni-cone Day.

Baby G: What does mythical mean?

Summer: When something or someone appears in or is described in a myth or folktale, they are not real, they are mythical. Myths talk about humans with supernatural, not from nature, powers, and fantastic beasts. They are imaginary. They only exist in stories or someone's imagination. The ancient Greeks and Romans believed in mythical gods such as Zeus, or Jupiter. Some myths start with something real, then people imagine something different.

Baby G: Did unicorns start with something real?

Summer: Maybe. The unicorn myths may be based on real rhinos. Some rhinos have one horn, but they don't look like horses, and don't have flowing manes and long tails. But an ancient species of rhinos, now extinct, was shaggy, and had slender legs like horses do.

Baby G: What do rhinos look like?

Summer: The word rhino is short for rhinoceros. The prefix rhino- means nose. The suffix -ceros means horn. Rhinos are the second largest land mammals. Elephants are the largest. The rhino is heavy, with a broad chest, and has thick, sturdy legs. There are five species of rhinos: two from Africa, and three from Asia. Some have one horn, and some have two. Their skin is very thick, like armor plating.

Willie: During the day, the rhino takes off its armor, and shines it up. When you see a rhino at night, is it a night in shining armor? 😂

Summer: Willie! Rhinos don't actually wear armor! Their thick skin protects them. Knights in shining armor are humans wearing armor, not rhinos. Baby, rhinos are very nearsighted, but have excellent hearing. They may charge into things they cannot see well, like trees or large rocks. A group of rhinos is called a crash. Like giraffes, the number of rhinos in the wild is dropping fast.

Baby G: World, you don't have to be in the USA or the UK to celebrate unicorns today. Happy National Unicorn Day! Please help the rhinos in the wild, their numbers are dropping fast. We don't want them to go the way of the unicorn, and only exist in stories.

Baby G: Mama, what is abuse?
Willie: An A-use is the best use of something. A B-use, or abuse, is the second-best use. The A-use of carrots is to eat them, and a B-use is to throw them away. Don't do that. Don't abuse anything or anyone. Don't abuse carrots. 😂
Summer: Willie, that is not what abuse means! And you are thinking of an A-list and a B-list. But you are right, don't abuse anything or anyone, even carrots. Baby G, abuse means you hurt someone you are supposed to take care of. It also means you misuse something, you use it in the wrong way, or for the wrong reasons. If you take illegal drugs, that is drug abuse. An A-list is a list of the most sought-after people. It usually is a list of actors or actresses or celebrities. The B-list has less desirable or famous people.
Baby G: Why would anyone abuse someone else? That is not nice.
Summer: It is not nice, and people who do it are evil or sick. The ones who do it are called abusers. The ones being abused are called victims. Abusers often tell their victims that the victims deserve to be abused because of something they did, or who they are. That is not true. No one deserves to be abused ever. Abusers tell their victims what happened is a secret, and if the victims ever tell anyone what happened, they will be hurt even more, or others will be abused too. Break the cycle of abuse. Tell someone you trust about the abuse, let them help you stop the abusers from ever doing it to you, or anyone else, ever again. Child abusers hurt children. Abusers may go after anyone who is smaller and weaker than them, or who may not be able to fight back, not just children. If they go after their mates, that is spousal abuse. If they go after old people, the elderly, that is elder abuse. If they go after animals, that is animal abuse. All abuse is wrong, but very young children and animals cannot speak for themselves. They cannot tell anyone what happened. They need you to help prevent abuse by raising awareness. April is National Child Abuse Prevention Month.
Willie: Are you aware you already said April is National Autism Awareness Month? No do-overs! 😂
Summer: Willie, it is both. There are many things that you should be aware of, and only twelve months in a year. So, each month has

multiple things to be aware of. Baby, spanking a misbehaving young child is not abuse. Older misbehaving children can be punished without spanking them. They can be sent to their rooms, or lose the use of something they enjoy, like a phone or computer. However, young children don't understand what older children do. They can badly hurt themselves while misbehaving, like if they try to touch a hot stove, after being told not to. Parents should use their hands, not a brush or belt, to spank young kids, so that they don't really hurt the child. They will hurt their own hand if they spank too hard. Willie: I use my neck to spank your mama. I can't use my hands, since giraffes don't have hands. I can't send her to her room, even though she is older. That's because she is already there with you. Summer: Willie! You aren't spanking me! Giraffes use their necks on each other as part of their mating dance. And stop calling me old! Baby G: World, April is National Child Abuse Prevention Month. If you are being abused, find someone you trust, and tell them what happened. Don't listen to your abuser when they say you deserve it or tell you to keep the secret. Break the cycle of abuse. Help young children and animals that are being abused. They cannot speak for themselves.

Comfort Animal

Tasha Poochette

Baby G: Mama, what is a comfort animal?

Summer: Baby G, an emotional support animal, or comfort animal, provides comfort and companionship to someone with a physical, mental, or emotional disability. It is usually a dog but can be another animal.

Baby G: What is comfort?

Summer: When you are relaxed, free from pain or constraint, you are comfortable. If you help someone feel better, or you ease their grief, or you make them less sad, you comfort them.

Willie: Son, make me more comfortable in my man cave. Bring me beer and carrots. We can relax and watch the lady giraffes at Cheyenne Mountain Zoo compete to get one lucky bull giraffe's attention. I wish I was that lucky. 😂

Summer: Willie! Giraffes don't have man caves, and don't drink beer! He is much too young to watch that, and you are just too much, to watch that show around me!

Baby G: What is a man cave?

Summer: A man cave is a room or area of a house, where the males can get away from the females, and relax. It usually has a TV. It may have other things like pool tables, pinball machines, video game systems, computers, etc. The males do hobbies, or other things they enjoy. Females have she sheds, which are very similar to man caves, but may have different games. The females may enjoy the same things as the males or enjoy different ones.

Willie: Giraffes don't shed hair. Can a female giraffe have a she shed if she doesn't shed? 😂

Summer: Willie, the word shed has multiple meanings. Baby, remember, if you shed hair, some of your hair falls out, and lands on the ground, or on the furniture. A shed is a small storage building.

Baby G: Are comfort animals pets?

Summer: Some comfort animals are also pets, but not all. Anyone can adopt a pet. But if you want an emotional support animal, and you live or travel where pets aren't allowed, a doctor or other medical professional needs to provide a note stating that you have a real disability, and an emotional support animal provides a benefit that helps you cope with your disability. Sometimes, people with or without disabilities feel better if they see us. They consider us to be their comfort animals.

Willie: Summer, come be my comfort animal. It makes me feel better if I see you, and even better if I can feel you. 😂

Summer: Willie, it will make me feel better if you get comfortable and let us talk. Baby, comfort animals are not trained like service animals. They cannot go everywhere like service animals can. Service animals are trained to help people do things. Guide dogs help the blind by seeing things the blind cannot see. They help a blind person safely cross a busy street. Hearing dogs help deaf people by listening for sounds, like a smoke alarm, that the deaf cannot hear. Seizure detection dogs help people with epilepsy. Post-Traumatic Stress Disorder (PTSD) dogs help soldiers and other military people cope with life after they return home. All service dogs are working animals, and not pets. But when they are at home, and their working gear or harness is off, they can play like pets.

Baby G: World, don't bother a service animal while it is at work. It has an important job to do. If you need us to be your comfort animals, we are glad to help you feel better.

Baby G: Mama, what are the rights to life, liberty and the pursuit of happiness?

Willie: I want to pursue a lady giraffe named Happy, but your mama won't let me. I guess I don't have the right to the single life, or the liberty to pursue Happy. 😂

Summer: Willie! You don't have the right to the single life because you aren't single! Baby G, in the USA, everyone has certain rights that God gave them, and which cannot be taken away. Among them are the rights to life, liberty, and the pursuit of happiness. Our country's laws are based on a document called the U.S. Constitution. There are other rights, such as freedom of speech, which are listed as amendments, changes, to the U.S. Constitution. The first ten amendments are called the Bill of Rights. An amendment can be repealed, taken away, but it is very hard to do it. That is good, because the rights listed in amendments never should be taken away either.

Baby G: What is liberty?

Willie: Lady Liberty is another lady giraffe I would like to pursue... 😂

Summer: Willie, Lady Liberty is not a giraffe! Baby, Lady Liberty is a large statue on an island in New York harbor. She carries a book of laws in her left hand and holds up a burning torch in her right hand. She represents friendship between nations and freedom. Liberty means you have the freedom to live where you want within your own country, and you have the right to live how you want, provided you don't hurt anyone. But a part of that is the right to LIVE. No one should be killed because of what they believe, or what color their skin is, or where they were born, or who their ancestors were. No one is better or worse than anyone else because of those things. No one who hasn't committed a crime should be put in jail or be held somewhere against their will. No one is guaranteed happiness. However, everyone has the right to discover what makes them happy, and go do it, so long as they don't do anything illegal, or step on someone's rights while doing it.

Willie: We are giraffes. We are tall. Humans are short, compared to us. We have hooves as big as dinner plates. It is hard enough not to step on the little people, no less their rights. 😂

Summer: Willie, that expression, "don't step on someone's rights", means don't do anything to violate or limit their rights. They have the same rights as you. Baby, everyone, human or giraffe, is equal in the USA. Not everyone had these rights in the beginning, but they do now.

Baby G: Do people in other countries also have these rights?

Summer: Not all do, but they should. People are fighting now to get the rights you have.

Baby G: So, these rights cannot be taken away once people get them?

Summer: That is how it is supposed to be. But there have been bad periods in history, both here and in other countries, where people lost their lives, or their liberty, because of what they believe, or what color their skin is, or where they were born, or who their ancestors were. We need to make sure that never happens again. Today is Jewish Holocaust Remembrance Day. Those that remember it need to remember, "Never Again".

Baby G: World, everyone should have the rights to life, liberty, and the pursuit of happiness. If your country doesn't give you these rights, fight for them. If you do have these rights, make sure they are never taken away.

Baby G: Mama, is the party all over?

Summer: Baby G, people all over the whole world are celebrating your first yearly birthday. Happy Birthday Baby G.

Baby G: Thanks, Mama. But I meant, is my party all done, is it finished?

Summer: No, your party is just getting started. The cake and hay table are gone. So is the wall banner. The people that were in our barn have left. But the people watching us on the live cam are partying on, and they are donating to our park. They are helping us help the giraffes in the wild, who won't have many more birthdays if something isn't done.

Baby G: I first thought the party was over when I knocked the hay table over. I didn't mean to knock it over.

Summer: We didn't see that because Daddy and I were put outside. But the live cam and chat were archived, so we can watch your birthday party over and over again. So can the world.

Willie: It is a father's duty to help his son. They should have let me in, so I could show you the object of the game is not to play ring around the hay table, or to knock it down. The object is to EAT.

😂

Summer: Willie, he figured it out on his own. Baby, now that you are older, you will figure more out on your own, and have new and exciting experiences. We know that you didn't mean to knock the hay table over. You were just very excited. No harm was done. Our human family set it back up, and you went for round two.

Baby G: I went round and round it during round two. Then I realized there was lettuce and other good things to eat on the hay table. I also saw myself on the banner on the wall and read my birthday message. Outside of our pen is another wall, it had many colors on it. What were those?

Summer: Those were birthday cards the world sent to our park. They wished you a happy first birthday, and some had donations in them.

Baby G: After a while, our human family moved the hay table, and let you and Daddy in. I am glad you two got to come to part of my party, but not so glad Daddy ate all of the leftovers!

Willie: It is a shame to waste food. When I was your age, we walked through the snow for miles to get to a birthday party, and ... 😂
Summer: Willie! You are only five years older than he is, and giraffes don't walk in snow! Baby, yeah, Daddy doesn't like people much. Sometimes, when someone comes to a birthday party, they are shy, or feel awkward about being with a lot of people. They may hang out near the food. Eating may make them feel better.
Willie: Eating always makes me feel better. We should keep giving him birthday parties, so we can all eat more birthday leftovers. Instead of celebrating his birthday once a month, how about we do it once a day? 😂
Summer: Willie, he is a year old. He is a yearling. Now he will celebrate his birthday once a year, not once a month, and certainly not once a day! Baby, you should make an extra effort to welcome everyone to your party, and if they just want to eat, and be left alone, let them know that is okay. Let them know you are glad they came.
Baby G: World, thanks for coming to my birthday party. I am one year old! If you are shy, you don't have to say much. Enjoy the food. I am so glad you came!

Baby G: Mama, what is procrastination?
Willie: When you are really good at something, you are a pro at it. When you are really good at being crass, and you live in a nation of people just like you, it is a pro-crass-nation. 😂
Summer: Willie, that is not what procrastination means! Baby G, your daddy is a pro at taking words and twisting their meanings, so he can make a joke. He is really good at it. The word 'pro' is short for professional, someone who is really good at something. Pro also means you are for something, you want it to happen. The opposite of 'pro' is 'con'. It means you are against something, you don't want it to happen. If you make a list of the pros and cons, reasons for doing something and reasons for not doing it, that helps you decide whether it is worth doing.
Willie: I have a pro and pro list about eating carrots. That is always worth doing. There are no cons, unless you try to con me out of my carrots! 😂
Summer: Willie, no one is trying to con you out of your carrots! Baby, a con is the act of deceiving or tricking someone, usually so you can steal something from them. You lie to them to persuade them to do something, or you get them to believe something that is not true. If you are convicted of any crime, like deliberately hurting or killing someone, or stealing something, you will go to jail. You become a convict.
Baby G: Do you ever get out of jail? Some people say we are in jail and should be let out.
Summer: We aren't in jail. We didn't commit any crimes. We are kept inside when the weather outside is bad, or it is nighttime. Even when it is nice outside, and the door is wide open, sometimes we choose to stay in. If you are a convict, you have no choices, you must do what the jailer says to do. If you deliberately hurt or kill someone, you may be in jail for life. For other crimes, you serve your time, then get to leave. After you leave jail, you will be an ex-con for the rest of your life. It is very hard to ever put that behind you and have a good life. Don't do the crime in the first place. Don't hurt or kill people, steal things, or con anyone out of anything.

Willie: If I eat late, my stomach growls at me. It says eat now, or you will die of hunger, and there will be a deadline, a chalk mark on the ground, in the shape of a skinny giraffe. 😂

Summer: Willie! You are in no danger of dying of hunger, and a deadline isn't a chalk mark! Baby, a deadline is the date or time by when you must finish something. If you procrastinate, you do something at the very last minute. You wait so long to do it, you may miss the deadline. Procrastination is the act of delaying, postponing, or avoiding what you must do until you are forced to do it. In the USA, Tax Day is usually April 15. This year, it is today, April 17. Adults must gather their records, fill out tax forms, and send them. They have months before the deadline to do that. But procrastinators wait until a few days before Tax Day to do their taxes. Some wait until hours before the taxes are due to do them. You shouldn't wait that long. It is very stressful to rush to do something, and in the rush, you may make mistakes. If you procrastinate while doing homework, and don't turn it in by the deadline, you may get a failing grade. Don't avoid what you must do. Avoid procrastination instead.

Baby G: World, don't procrastinate. Don't wait until the last minute to do something. If you rush, it is very stressful, you may make mistakes, and you may miss your deadline. Don't con anyone out of anything.

Baby G: Mama, what are animal crackers?

Willie: I crack jokes, and I am an animal. Therefore, I am an animal cracker. 😂

Summer: Willie, you are not an animal cracker, but there are giraffe animal crackers. Baby G, today is April 18. It is National Animal Crackers Day. Animal crackers are cookies that are animal shaped. They look like animals, especially zoo or circus animals. They aren't actually crackers but are called that because they are crunchy. In the UK, cookies are called biscuits. In the USA, biscuits are small, baked, bread cakes. They are flaky and chewy. They are served with butter or fruit jam. Cookies are small, flat cakes. They are usually sweet, because they contain sugar. They can be hard, thin and crunchy, or soft, thick and chewy. Crackers are thin, crisp, flat wafers. They are not usually sweet, but they are often served with something on top, which may be sweet or savory. Crackers are often served with cheese. Crackers are crunchy.

Baby G: Do animals eat cookies or biscuits or crackers?

Summer: We giraffes may get some crackers, especially as a reward for doing what our human family wants us to do. Dogs get hard, crunchy biscuits. Today is also World Heritage Day. People all over the world celebrate their heritage.

Willie: When humans are born, they have no hair. Then they grow some. As their hair ages, it falls out. They end up with no hair. While still young, they celebrate their hair-age. 😂

Summer: Willie, no one celebrates their hair-age! Baby, when you celebrate your heritage, you celebrate where your ancestors came from, and what traditions were passed down to you. You celebrate your culture. You raise awareness about historical monuments, and sites. You help protect and preserve them, no matter whether they are for a religion you don't believe, or they are in a place you don't live, or they are part of a history you don't share. You protect and preserve them because they are part of the world's history.

Baby G: What else is passed down?

Summer: Many things are passed down: recipes, foods, songs, music, dances, etc. Your parents may pass down a family photo album or scrapbook, a family cookbook full of favorite recipes, or a family Bible. Some things passed down are not things at all. They are ideas, about what things are important, what is good, what is bad, and what is worth protecting and preserving.

Willie: Son, my carrot stash will be yours someday. It is your inheritance. It is worth protecting, but not preserving.

The point of carrots is to eat them, not look at them. 🤣

Baby G: World, today is World Heritage Day. Think about what is worth protecting and preserving and enjoy a cookie or biscuit while thinking about that. Or maybe you can celebrate National Animal Crackers Day at the same time. What is your favorite animal?

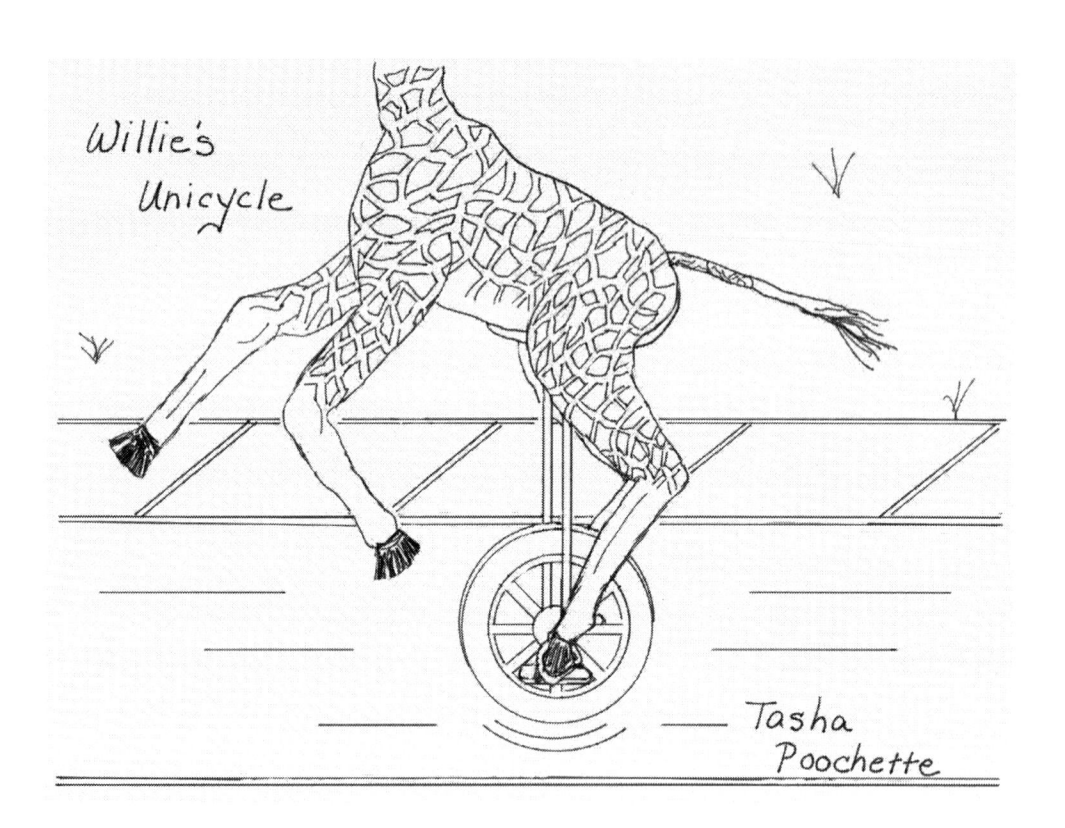

Baby G: Mama, what is a cycle?

Summer: Baby G, a cycle is something that happens over and over again. We have talked about the cycle of seasons, the cycle of abuse, and other cycles. The word 'cycle' is also short for bicycle.

Willie: The definition of insanity is doing the same thing over and over again and expecting different results. A fish on a bicycle is insane. He cannot reach the pedals, but he keeps trying. 😂

Summer: Willie, you are right, that is the definition of insanity. But a fish riding on a bicycle isn't insane. It just isn't possible. Baby, if someone needs something like a fish needs a bicycle, they don't need it at all, it is useless to them.

Baby G: What is a bicycle?

Summer: A bicycle is something with wheels. You sit on a seat, and hold the handle bars, and push the pedals with your feet. Then the wheels move round and round, they cycle, moving the bicycle forward or backward.

Baby G: Why is it called a bicycle?

Summer: The prefix bi- means two. The bicycle has two wheels.

Willie: I am unique, so of course I ride a unicycle. 😂

Summer: Willie! Giraffes cannot ride a cycle, no matter how many wheels it has! Baby, remember, the prefix uni- means one. A unicycle is like a bicycle, but only has one wheel. The prefix tri- means three. A tricycle is like a bicycle but has three wheels. The prefix quad- means four. A quadricycle or quad bike has four wheels. Riding a cycle, no matter how many wheels it has, is smart and a lot of fun, unless you are a fish or a giraffe. Humans ride cycles to exercise, to get somewhere, and just for the joy of it.

Baby G: Which cycle would a human prefer?

Summer: It depends on how old they are. A very young child rides a tricycle, because it is very stable, and won't tip over. An older child will ride a bicycle, with training wheels attached to keep it stable. After some practice balancing and riding the bicycle, the training wheels come off. Adults like bicycles too. If a bicycle has a motor to move it instead of pedals, it is a moped. If it has a bigger motor, it is a motorcycle. Some motorcycles have three wheels. Quad bikes also have motors, and are used off-road.

Baby G: What is off-road?

Summer: Sometimes it helps you understand what something is if you realize what it is not, what its opposite is. Off-road is the opposite of on-road. The wheels on any bike, no matter how many wheels it has, roll along the ground. Rubber tires or tyres, usually filled with air, and placed on the wheels, provide traction. The tires grip the ground, and don't slide. If the ground is very smooth and flat, like on a paved road, it is easier on the tires. The tires for an on-road bike are skinny. Off the road, the tires might be punctured by sharp rocks, or sink in gravel. So off-road bikes have wider, tougher tires, with less air in them, on their wheels. Off-road or mountain bikes go on dirt trails. Quad bikes also go on sand dunes.

Willie: I am tired of talking about tires. Let's retire this subject, and move on to one I never tire of: what foods do you never tire of? 😂

Baby G: World, don't do the same thing over and over again, and expect different results. That is insane. But riding a cycle is smart and a lot of fun, unless you are a fish or a giraffe. Where will you go?

Baby G: Mama, does God make mistakes?

Willie: Yeah, God makes mistakes. The time to make a baby giraffe is too long, and the time to enjoy a carrot is too short. I must bring my cud back up to enjoy it again. 😂

Summer: Willie, every type of animal takes a different amount of time to make a baby. It isn't too long or too short, it is what it is. Baby G, I don't think He does. But not everyone agrees with that. Let's look at what causes you to make mistakes and see if those reasons apply to God. You may make a mistake because you don't know any better, like when you write a word for the first time. You may use the wrong letters, or the right ones in the wrong order. You may make a spelling mistake. You may use the wrong word or put the right word in the wrong place in a sentence. You may make a grammatical error. You may make a mistake because you lack knowledge about how to do something, or you don't know what something is. God knows everything, so He would not make those kinds of mistakes. You may make a mistake because you are in too much of a hurry to finish something, or you are careless. God has all the time in the world. He is in no rush. If someone uses poor reasoning, they may start with true statements, and still come up with the wrong conclusion. If you were given only orange carrots in the past, you may reason this way: "I have a carrot, it is orange, my last carrot was also orange, therefore my next carrot will be orange." That is the wrong conclusion, because not all carrots are orange. Your next carrot could be yellow or some other color.

Willie: I am willing to eat all the yellow or other colored carrots, and then he won't make the wrong conclusion. His next carrot will be orange. 😂

Summer: Willie! Thanks, but no thanks. He doesn't need you to cover up his mistakes! He needs to learn and use better reasoning. Baby, God uses good reasoning, plus He knows what will happen, so He wouldn't make this kind of mistake. You may make a mistake and judge someone unfairly, because you don't know all the facts. You don't know what they were thinking or did. You may be biased against them because they are different than you. God knows what is in everyone's heart and loves everyone equally.

Baby G: Why do some people think God makes mistakes?
Summer: Some don't believe in Him. Some do believe, but feel because He allows suffering and pain, and allows people to die, that means He makes mistakes. There was a movie, where someone pretended to be God, and said He made one mistake: He made the pits in avocados too big. Ever since the lady who writes about us saw that movie, she has asked people, "If you were God, what 'mistake' would you fix?" People need to die. Our Earth couldn't feed everyone if the population got too big. It would get too big if people didn't die. Pain is your body's way of telling you to stop doing what you are doing, you are hurting yourself. Suffering enables you to learn you can get through anything with God's help, it makes you stronger. So, suffering, pain, and people dying aren't actually mistakes. But once you get the message to stop doing what you are doing, pain just hurts. If that lady were God, she would eliminate all pain after the initial pain, because she doesn't want people to hurt.
Willie: No mistake about it, I want people to laugh at my jokes until it hurts, so don't be a pain, and not laugh. 😂
Baby G: World, do you think God makes mistakes? If you were God, what 'mistake' would you fix?

Baby G: Mama, if we didn't live on Earth, where would we live?

Willie: I want to live on Venus. I hear it is warm there. I am tired of winter weather. It is supposed to be springtime! 😂

Summer: Willie, it is too hot on Venus for anyone or anything to live there! Baby G, some people think we could live on another planet.

Baby G: What are planets?

Summer: Planets are round like a ball, but much bigger. They move around a star. The Earth we live on is a planet. It goes around a star we call the sun. There are eight planets that go around the sun.

Willie: There used to be nine planets, but the ninth one, Pluto, was a bad boy. He cut space class too often and got demoted a grade in school. 😂

Summer: Willie! Pluto wasn't a bad boy! However, you are right, Pluto was classified as a planet, but was downgraded to a dwarf planet or planetoid.

Baby G: What are the eight planets?

Summer: In order, from closest to the sun to furthest out, are Mercury, Venus, Earth, Mars, Jupiter, Saturn, Uranus, and Neptune.

Baby G: I thought Jupiter was a Roman god.

Summer: He was. Many of the planets, but not all, were named after Roman gods.

Baby G: Can we live on other planets?

Summer: Not without a lot of help. It takes a long time to get to another planet, and we would have to build something that would safely take us there. We would also have to build something that would enable us to live there.

Baby G: Like what?

Summer: We live on Earth because God, or nature, depending on what you believe, set up the things we need for life: light, air, infrared radiation (heat), and water. You can use the acronym LAIR to remember that. L for light, A for air, I for Infrared radiation (heat), and last but not least, the word water ends with the letter R. Other planets are too hot or too cold, too dark or too bright, or don't have air to breathe, or don't have water to drink. We also need a way to grow food, we need a shelter or a way to build one, and we need to be able to sleep.

Baby G: What is an acronym?

Summer: An acronym is usually formed from the initial, first, letters of other words, but other letters can be used. It is pronounced like a word. In this case, it is pronounced like the word 'lair'.

Baby G: What is a lair?

Summer: A lair is a secret, hidden, or private place where someone lives or rests. It is a house for a human, a den for a bear or a wolf, etc. We all share one lair, the Earth. Today is April 22. It is Earth Day. We need to take care of our Earth. It enables us to live, and there is only one of it.

Willie: There is only one of me too. Help me live, by saving our Earth. 😂

Baby G: World, today is Earth Day. Take care of it. We need to live here, since we cannot live anywhere else, without a lot of help.

Baby G: Mama, what does it mean to paint a picture with words?

Willie: It means you run out of paint colors before you finish your painting, and you use some bad words, because you are upset. You paint your picture with words. 😂

Summer: Willie, that isn't what "painting a picture with words" means! Baby G, bad words are words you shouldn't use, because you are too young, or those words are rude, or they are wrong for anyone to say, no matter how old they are. Profanity, bad language, swear words, and choice words may offend other people. Don't use them, unless you are very upset, and cannot control yourself.

Willie: Yeah, if you must eat your words, and you use bad words, you may end up with a very upset stomach. 😂

Summer: Willie! That phrase, "eat your words", doesn't mean you actually eat them! It means you must admit that something you said in the past was wrong. Baby, even if you are very upset, try your hardest not to use bad words, and immediately apologize to everyone who heard you. When you paint a picture with words, you describe something, then the person listening to you, or reading your written words, can imagine it. They can see in their minds every detail of what you are describing.

Baby G: So, there is no actual picture?

Summer: In a book, there might be actual pictures or drawings, illustrations, along with written words. Books for young children usually have more pictures than words. Books for older children, teens, or adults usually have more words than pictures. Some have no pictures at all. Today is April 23. It is World Book Day. It celebrates authors, those people who write books and stories, and illustrators, those who create drawings and illustrations. It also celebrates books and reading.

Baby G: What kinds of books are there?

Summer: Fiction refers to books or stories that were created by someone using their imagination. They describe imaginary events, events that never happened; imaginary people, people who never existed; and imaginary places. Or they describe real people and real places, but those people in real life never actually visited those places or did those things. There are nonfiction books. Everything in those books really happened to people. Books can take you places in your mind, without you ever leaving home. Books describe real or imaginary places you have never been, and real or imaginary things you have never seen. You can lose yourself in a book.

Willie: I lost myself in a book. Then I couldn't find me. I had to reread the whole book to find myself. 😂

Summer: Willie, losing yourself in a book means you are unaware you are reading, you forget you are here, the book has taken you somewhere else in your mind. That is a wonderful thing. Baby, before you can lose yourself in a book, you need to practice reading. It is hard to be unaware, not know, you are reading, if reading is hard for you. Read many books and stories. Practice makes perfect. You can take a book with you, when you do leave home. Books are easy to carry. Even easier, put a book on a tablet or phone, and carry that with you.

Baby G: World, Happy World Book Day! Books can paint pictures with words. They describe places you have never been, and things you have never seen. Grab a book, and go somewhere in real life, or just in your mind. Where will you go?

Baby G: Mama, what is a school bus?

Summer: Baby G, a school bus takes children to school. A bus driver drives the school bus, and picks up kids near their homes, or at bus stops. Kids get on the bus and sit down in the many seats. After all the kids are on the bus, it takes them to school. After school is out, the bus takes them home again, or to their bus stops.

Baby G: Why don't I get to go on the school bus?

Summer: You are a giraffe. Even though you are little for a giraffe, at ten feet, you are much bigger than even the biggest human. You can't fit in a bus seat.

Baby G: Couldn't I stand in the back?

Summer: Standing in a moving school bus is not safe. Today is School Bus Drivers' Day. Every day, not just today, everyone needs to listen to the bus driver, and stay seated until the bus arrives at school, and the bus is stopped. Wish the bus driver a Happy School Bus Drivers' Day.

Willie: Aren't the school bus drivers happier when school is out for the summer? They won't have to deal with a bunch of noisy kids. Shouldn't that be Happy No School Day? 😂

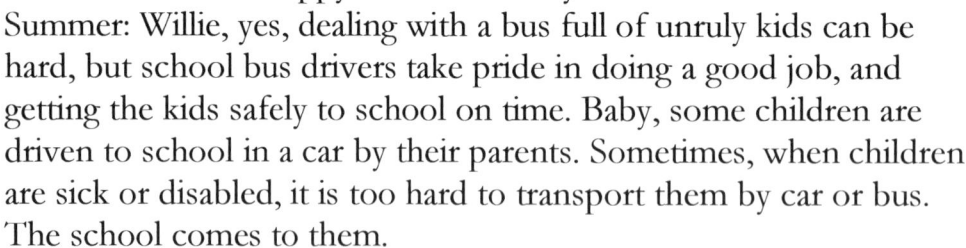

Summer: Willie, yes, dealing with a bus full of unruly kids can be hard, but school bus drivers take pride in doing a good job, and getting the kids safely to school on time. Baby, some children are driven to school in a car by their parents. Sometimes, when children are sick or disabled, it is too hard to transport them by car or bus. The school comes to them.

Willie: If you are a fish, you don't go to school and your school doesn't come to you. It goes with you wherever you go. 😂

Summer: Willie, a school of fish is a group of fish swimming together in a coordinated way. Baby, some children are well, but their parents still choose to teach them at home. Home schooled kids, like you, don't need to ride a bus to school, or be driven there. The parents get to decide what to teach their children, and when, where, and how to do lessons. The kids get individual attention from their parents, instead of being in a big class. Not all parents have the time or wish to teach their children at home. Some children have only one parent, and that parent may need to work. Children may benefit more from going to a regular school. They are taught by trained teachers, who know what their students need to learn, and how to teach them. Kids can make friends there, learn to play and work with people who are different from them, and participate in team sports. They may be better prepared to go to college later. In the USA, public schools are free to everyone, and paid for by the government, using tax money. Private schools cost parents money. Most parents cannot afford to send their kids to private schools. Some private schools are boarding schools, where children live at the schools, and only go home on holidays. Some parents don't want to be separated from their kids most of the year. Whether you are home schooled, take a school bus to school, are driven there, or live there, pay attention and learn. That is your most important job when you are a kid.

Willie: I am ready to be separated from my kid most of the year. Wait, I already am separated from him by the fence between our pens. 😂

Baby G: World, no matter where your school is, pay attention to your teachers. Remember, learning is your most important job when you are a kid. And if you do ride a school bus, wish your bus driver a Happy School Bus Drivers' Day.

Baby G: Mama, what does it mean to color outside the lines?

Willie: If you have two lines of penguins marching across the ice in their black-tie outfits, and one penguin, dressed in a plaid coat, marches to a different drummer, he is in color, outside the lines. 😂

Summer: Willie, that is not what "color outside the lines" means! Baby G, soldiers form lines, and they march together, while a drummer plays on a drum. Everyone does the same thing at the same time, or at the same beat of the drum. "Marching to a different drummer" means you go off and do something different than everyone else does. Coloring books have drawings of things in them. They may be drawings of animals, even giraffes. The drawings have lines around them. You are supposed to color, use a crayon or coloring pencil, inside the lines. If you color outside the lines, you are doing your own thing, you are not doing what everyone else is doing. And that is okay.

Baby G: What are penguins?

Summer: Penguins are flightless birds. They cannot fly, but they swim really well, using their wings like flippers. They have webbed feet. They have black upper parts and white underparts. They live in the southern hemisphere. Some live where it is very cold, where there is ice all year.

Baby G: What are black tie outfits?

Summer: When humans dress up for a formal dance or wedding, the men wear black bow ties with tuxedos. A tuxedo includes a dinner jacket, white formal shirt, cummerbund or waistcoat, and black pants. The women wear long formal dresses.

Willie: The men call that a monkey suit, but they look like penguins. Don't they know that the Reticulated giraffe pattern is better? I would rather look like a giraffe, than a penguin or a monkey. 😂

Summer: Willie! They don't look like monkeys! Although they do look a little like penguins because they are dressed in black and white.

Baby G: What is plaid?

Summer: Human clothes can be all one color, be multicolored, or have patterns, with certain lines or repeated colors. There are plaids, polka dots, stripes, leopard spots, and other patterns. Some clothes even have giraffe patterns on them.

Baby G: What are crayons?

Summer: Crayons are little wax or chalk sticks that come in different colors. In the USA, the Crayola company makes the most popular crayons. March 31 was National Crayon Day. Today is April 25. It is National Crayola Day. It is also World Penguin Day. Celebrate both by coloring a picture of penguins.

Baby G: Do I have to color them black and white?

Summer: Color outside of the lines and make them any color you want.

Willie: Do old penguins color their grey hairs black or white? 😂

Summer: Willie, animals don't dye their hair, no matter how old they are! Some humans dye their pets' hair. That is so embarrassing for them. But the pets love their human families and put up with that nonsense to make them happy.

Baby G: World, Happy World Penguin Day. Learn about these birds while coloring them. Don't be afraid to color outside the lines and do your own thing. March to a different drummer.

Baby G: Mama, what is the home stretch?
Willie: You are at home, and you do yoga stretches. That is the home stretch. Because we are giraffes, and we have long necks, we can really stretch. 😂
Summer: Willie, everything you just said is true, yet it is totally irrelevant. Baby G, something is irrelevant when it has nothing to do with what you are doing, or what you want to know. If you join a conversation, make sure what you have to say is relevant. If it isn't relevant, you can wait your turn, then start your own chat about anything you want. The home stretch has nothing to do with being at home, or doing yoga stretches. When you are almost finished with something, you are on the home stretch. You are in the last part, the final stage.
Baby G: Why is that called the home stretch?
Summer: When horses compete in a race, they run around a racetrack. The track is oval shaped. It has two straight sides and curves at the ends. The horses finish their race on a straight side of the track. That is the home stretch. It is the part of the track between the last turn and the finish line.
Baby G: What is a stage?
Willie: "All the world's a stage, And all the men and women merely players; They have their exits and their entrances ...". 😂
Summer: Willie! Get off the stage, make your exit, and let us talk. Baby, a stage is a raised platform in a theatre or school, where actors, comedians, speakers, and other people perform. A stage is also one part of a series of steps required to do something. You divide the activity into parts, and do each part, or stage, separately. A stagecoach was a horse-drawn, covered carriage with four wheels. It carried people and mail along a regular route between towns or

cities. The word 'carriage' is based on the word 'carry'. When you carry someone or something, you support their or its weight, and move them or it from one place to another. The tortoises in our loft didn't get there on their own. They cannot climb stairs. They were carried there by our human family.

Baby G: Can giraffes be carried, or carry anything?

Summer: Giraffes are way too heavy to be carried by a human, but can be put in, or on, a truck, van or train, and carried or moved to a new home. When you were a few weeks old, you were carried while you were weighed, but you were much smaller and lighter then. You are now one and three quarters times as tall, and eight times as heavy. Our backs are not really suited to carrying anyone or anything, although tickbirds sometimes ride on us. Horses, camels, and elephants do carry humans.

Willie: Your mama carried you for sixteen months before you were born. You were only supposed to be carried for fifteen months. Then she wanted to take a load off and rest her feet. So, she evicted you from the premises. 😂

Summer: Willie, he was born, not evicted from the premises! Baby, that saying, "take a load off", means sit down and relax. It also means don't worry about anything.

Baby G: World, if you are on the home stretch of anything, congratulations, you are almost done. When you finish, come watch us, and take a load off. If you join a conversation, make sure what you have to say is relevant. If it isn't relevant, you can wait your turn, then start your own chat about anything you want.

Baby G: Mama, what does it mean to come out of your shell?
Willie: Today is April 27. It is National Tell A Story Day. Let me tell you a story. There was a tortoise in our loft. He worked hard, doing whatever it is that tortoises do. He heard that his fellow workers like to party in the loft, and watch us on the live cam, instead of working. They lurk while they pretend to work. They "wurk". He wanted to party with them, but he was very shy. A lady tortoise told him to come out of his shell, and dance with her on it. His shell cracked, and he fell over. A lampshade landed on his head. His boss fired him. Now he is jobless and homeless too. The moral of the story is: Don't party too hard when at work. You may end up jobless and homeless, with a lampshade as your only cover. 😂
Summer: Willie, that is a fantastic story! Baby G, if you "come out of your shell", that doesn't mean you literally come out of a shell. Tortoises and turtles may poke their heads, arms and legs out of their shells, but they cannot actually leave their shells, or dance on them.
Willie: If I had a shell, I would use it to eat my carrots in private and hide from people. But my shell would have a Reticulated giraffe pattern, not a tortoise shell pattern. 😂
Summer: Willie, you often use our barn like a shell, as a way to hide from people. You would get more carrots if you didn't hide. Be friendly to more people. Baby, if someone tells you to "come out of your shell", they want you to meet more people, be friendly, not to be shy, join the party.
Baby G: What is a moral of a story?
Summer: The moral of a story is a life lesson you learn by reading or hearing the story. Remember, life lessons teach you how to live a better life. They give you useful information and teach you about principles and values. They teach you morals, what is right and what is wrong to do.
Baby G: If you are fired from your job, can't you just get another job?
Summer: Not always. You need to know certain things, have certain skills, to get and hold certain jobs. You need a way to get to the job, via a car or bus. Sometimes, jobs are hard to find, and a lot of other

people may compete with you for the few jobs available. Plus, if a new employer hears about why you lost your old job, he may not want to hire you for a new job. If you have no job, you may run out of money, and become homeless.
Willie: He has no job, he has no money, when will he be homeless?

I need more room for my man cave! 😂
Summer: Willie! He has no job, because he is a child, and no money, because he is a giraffe! He doesn't need them, because our human family takes care of us. Whether this is his forever home, or he goes somewhere else to have a family of his own, he will never be homeless! Being homeless is no joke. People suffer in the rain and the cold.
Baby G: Where do the homeless people go?
Summer: Sometimes, they go to a homeless shelter. Sometimes, they live in cars. Sometimes, they live on the street, and beg you for money. It is dangerous there. If you want to help, don't donate to people begging for money on the street. You don't want to encourage beggars. Instead, donate money and things they need, like blankets and clothes, to a homeless shelter.
Baby G: World, if you are shy, come out of your shell, and join the party. We are celebrating National Tell A Story Day. But don't party too much at work. You don't want to become jobless and homeless. Help those who are by donating to homeless shelters.

Baby G: Mama, what does "it is not my fault" mean?
Willie: The San Andreas fault is in California. I am in New York. It is not my fault. 😂
Summer: Willie, it is your fault that you are confusing two different meanings of the word 'fault'. Baby G, when you do or say something wrong, or you make a mistake, you caused it. You are responsible for it. It is your fault. If you don't know it is wrong, it is still your fault, but we will not blame you. You don't know any better. When an earthquake happens, it is usually along a fault line. A fault is a crack, an opening in the Earth. Rocks on either side of the fault slide past each other, or move apart, or one side slides over the other side.
Baby G: I don't understand.
Summer: Stand by me. We will face opposite directions, with our sides touching.
Baby G: Okay.
Summer: There is no gap, no opening, between us. Now step forward. I will do that too. We are moving in opposite directions, while still touching each other. We are sliding past each other. Start again. This time, we will step sideways. We are moving apart. There is now a gap between us. Start again. This time I will go down, I will lay down. Put your foot on me, like you do when you want me to get up so that you can get to the "milk bar". Now slide your hoof over me. You are sliding over me. The ground shakes during an earthquake. Buildings, bridges, people, and animals may fall down or get hurt or be killed. During an earthquake, drop down onto your hands and knees, or if you have no hands, lay down. Cover yourself with a table or desk, if one is nearby. If not, stand in a doorway. Try to hold on to something. You or your parents can prepare

ahead of time for earthquakes, by putting extra food, water, clothes, shoes, flashlights or torches, batteries, radios, medicines, blankets, pet food, etc. in a container somewhere in your barn, house, or garage. Plan how to get out, and where to go. April is Earthquake Preparedness Month. It is also Parkinson's Awareness Month.

Willie: Today is April 30. It is the last day of the month. How can I be prepared? You gave me only one day! 😂

Summer: Willie, you have all year to prepare for earthquakes, and to learn about Parkinson's disease. Baby, someone with Parkinson's disease moves slowly. Their movements are not easy and smooth. They are stiff. They may shake. They may lose their balance and fall down. They may have problems walking or smiling or thinking or talking. They may get depressed or anxious.

Willie: If someone with Parkinson's disease quakes with fear, or shakes during an earthquake, how can you tell? 😂

Summer: Willie! Don't make fun of someone with Parkinson's disease! They cannot control their shakes. Baby, none of their symptoms is their fault. Help someone deal with this horrible disease and make others aware they need help.

Baby G: World, be aware people with Parkinson's disease need help. Don't make fun of them. They cannot control their shakes. But you can control how you prepare for earthquakes.

"Take time to smell the carrot roses"

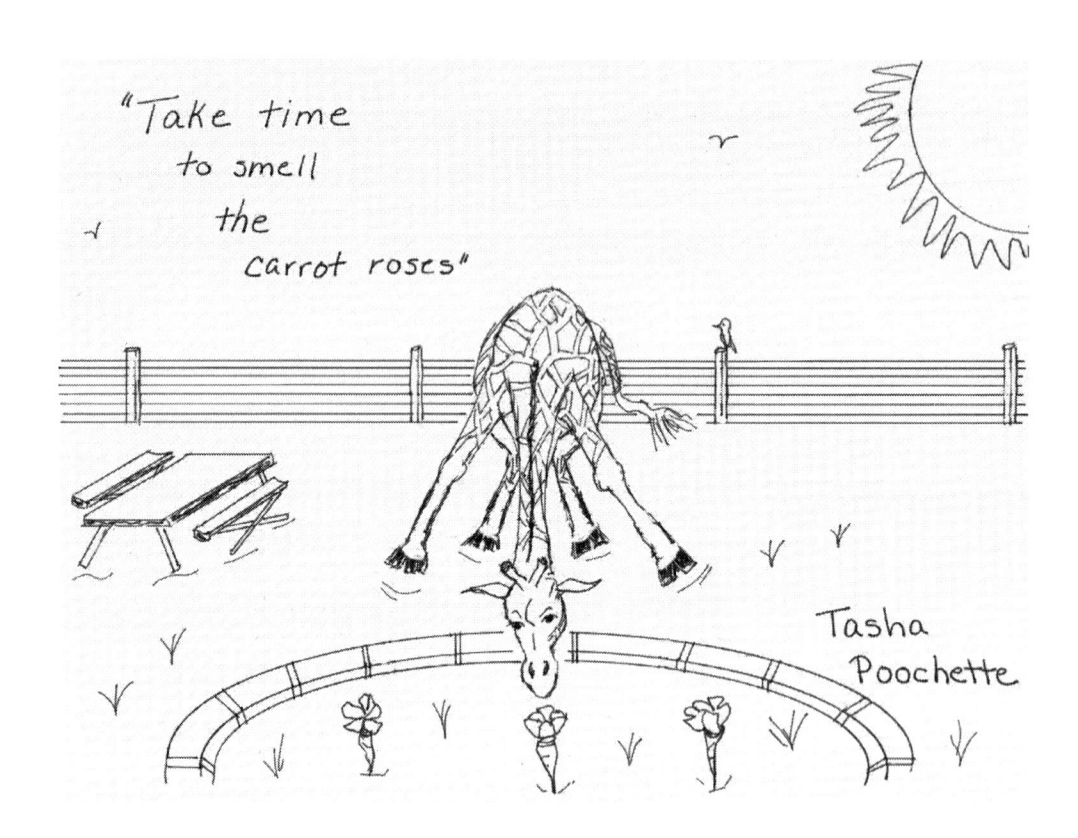

Tasha Poochette

Baby G: Mama, what is May Day?

Willie: When I am chased by humans trying to kiss me, I get scared, and yell, "May Day! Save me!" 😂

Summer: Willie, that is not what "May Day" means! A mayday is a radio distress signal, a cry for help. If your boat is sinking, or your airplane is in trouble, you say "Mayday" three times in a row: Mayday, Mayday, Mayday. You only do it in a true emergency, not when you don't want to be kissed! Baby G, today is May 1. It is May Day in many countries. It is a celebration of spring, with dancing, singing and food. There is a saying, "April showers bring May flowers". The rain that fell in the month of April helps plants to grow, and they produce flowers. Sometimes, people dance around a May pole, which is decorated with flowers and long ribbons. Some hang a May basket of flowers and candy on the front door of a house, which indicates they like, or are interested in, the person living there. Some celebrate spring by giving flowers to each other.

Baby G: Why do they give flowers?

Summer: Flowers are pretty, and some smell good. There is a saying, "take time to smell the flowers". Another version of it is, "stop and smell the roses". It means don't be so busy doing things you have to do, you forget to enjoy doing them, or forget to enjoy just being alive. Some flowers are even edible, you can eat them. Some "flowers" are foods that have been cut, or arranged, to look like flowers.

Willie: I want those kinds of flowers! Carrot roses, lettuce leaves, ... You don't have to limit them to May Day. I want to take time all year to smell the carrot roses, enjoy being alive, and get busy eating them. 😂

Summer: Willie, people can give flowers all year, whether they are real flowers, or they are "flowers" made from food. But people really like to do it on holidays. Baby, people give flowers to show they care about someone. Even though the flowers wilt, they only stay nice for a short time, they represent a long-lasting love or friendship. When you buy flowers for someone, you are saying you are willing to spend your money on something that doesn't last, just because that person loves getting them. Some countries celebrate International Workers' Day today. It is like our Labor Day. The workers are given the day off.

Willie: Do the flower workers get the day off too? Where do you get the flowers to give each other, if nobody is working at the flower market? Do you pick the flowers yourself? Which means you are working, when you aren't supposed to be working. Figuring this out is too much work. I will give my brain the day off. 😂

Summer: Willie, it is like any other holiday. Some people work on holidays, especially people who work in flower markets, grocery stores, retail stores, restaurants, or in entertainment. They make the holiday nice for those who do get the day off. They may get paid extra money for working on a holiday. They may get their own day off later, on what would normally be a working day for them.

Baby G: World, today is May Day. It is also International Workers' Day. Take time to smell the flowers.

Baby G: Mama, what does "don't be such a baby" mean?
Willie: Don't be such a baby. Grow up, and get out of here, so we can replace you with another baby, your younger brother or sister. 😂

Summer: Willie, new babies are not replacements for old ones! There is plenty of room, and plenty of love to go around! Baby G, today is May 2. It is Baby Day. It is also Brothers and Sisters Day. When someone says, "don't be such a baby", they mean you shouldn't whine or cry like a human baby, if you don't get what you want, when you want it. Rarely, baby giraffes can vocalize, make sounds humans can hear, when they are upset, or they want their mamas. They lose that ability. It takes human babies a while to learn to do anything, including talk. They cannot tell their parents what they want. They can only cry, until their parents figure out what is wrong: the babies are hungry, want to be held, their diapers need changing, etc. Humans usually don't learn to walk until they are a year old. You were walking forty-five minutes after you were born.
Willie: I am a proud papa. My baby got off to a fast start. I'd be prouder, if he grew up fast too. 😂
Summer: Willie! He is growing up too fast as it is. Enjoy him at every age, or stage, of his life. Baby, wild animals need to be able to run or swim away from predators soon after they are born. All animals grow up faster than humans. You will start making a family of your own by the time you are three or four years old. Humans can't be on their own until they are eighteen. Animal lives are usually much shorter than human lives. Someone said pet lives are shorter than human lives, by design, so pets will never have to worry about having someone to take care of them. Some tortoises, sponges, sea urchins, clams, lizards, worms, fish, whales, and jellyfish live longer than humans do. There is a jellyfish which doesn't die from old age. It still can die, if it gets hurt or sick, or is hunted by a predator.
Baby G: Do humans want to grow up?
Summer: When you are a child, your parents make sure you have food, water, clothes, and shelter. The downside is you are told what to do, and when to do it. After you grow up, unlike a baby, you can

say what you want, and unlike a child, you get to do what you want, when you want. The downside is usually you must work to get money and pay bills for everything. Some adults get tired of working, but they are too young to retire. They would love it if someone else took care of them. Someone joked about how they tried adulthood, it is not for them, and now they just want to get into their pajamas, make a blanket fort, and color. No one can actually be a young child, or even a baby, again. Besides, they wouldn't want to be told what to do, and when to do it, or be unable to say what they want, and only be able to whine or cry. Willie: I don't want to be told what to do, and when to do it. I reserve the right to whine and cry when people don't do what I want, when I want. I want carrots, and I want them NOW! 😂
Summer: Willie, act your age, and be friendlier to your fans. Then, they will do what they want, when they want: give you more carrots. They will do it to make you happy, not because they were told to do it.
Baby G: World, today is Baby Day. It is also Brothers and Sisters Day. Babies cannot tell you what they want. Children are told what to do, and when to do it. Adults usually must work and pay bills. Every age has its downside. Enjoy whatever age you are, at least you are alive!

Baby G: Mama, what is wordplay?
Summer: Baby G, wordplay is the clever use of certain words in writing or in conversations. You choose words both based on what they mean, and what other words they sound like. Your daddy loves wordplay, and often uses it in his jokes.
Baby G: I don't understand.
Summer: I might say, "I was late today because I got stuck behind a tower of lady giraffes standing in the middle of the road". Your daddy would say ...

Willie: She was late because she was stuck in a giraffic jam. 😂
Baby G: Why is that wordplay?
Summer: A traffic jam is a bunch of vehicles, cars and trucks, that are not moving, or are moving very slowly. A traffic jam happens after an accident, or when there is something blocking the road, or where there is road construction, people are working on the road, or when there are too many vehicles on that road. If that happens to you, then you are stuck in a traffic jam. Your daddy used a pun when he referred to the "giraffic jam". The road was jammed, filled, with giraffes. It was a pun, because traffic jam and giraffic jam sound alike, and sort of, but not really, have the same meaning. Wordplay includes puns, spoonerisms, odd or old meanings for words, twisted words, words with double meanings, made-up words, rhymes, etc.
Baby G: What are spoonerisms?
Summer: When you switch parts of two words in a phrase and come up with two new words that sort of rhyme with the original words, that is a spoonerism.

Willie: That spoonerism is a spat thoonerism. 😂
Summer: Willie, the new words must make sense. For example, "The Lord is a loving shepherd" becomes "The Lord is a shoving leopard".
Baby G: When do you do wordplay?
Summer: Wordplay shows up in lots of places, like in jokes, or in witty conversations, in stories and books, and in crossword puzzles.
Baby G: What are those?

Summer: A crossword puzzle is a grid, a bunch of black or white squares. You need to figure out what letter goes into each white square. The letters you put in the white squares form words. The words are written across or down. The black squares separate the words. Some of the white squares contain numbers. There is a clue for each number. The clues help you figure out what words to use. The clues use wordplay. Today is May 3. It is Wordsmith Day. A wordsmith is someone who has a way with words, they are a skilled user of words, or they are paid to work with words, like a writer or journalist or crossword puzzle maker. They play with words.

Willie: I play with words all the time. Where is my pay? I want pay-to-play! 😂

Summer: Willie! Giraffes are not paid for anything! Your jokes are a labor of love. You do them because you love to do them, not for pay. Besides, pay-to-play means someone must pay to take part in something, or to get favors. That payment may be illegal, in which case, you are participating in a pay-to-play scandal. Don't do that.

Baby G: World, Happy Wordsmith Day. Let's play with words!

Baby G: Mama, what does "for the birds" mean?
Willie: If you plant carrot seeds in the ground, cover them with soil, water them, and wait, carrot plants will grow. The carrots are for you. If you fail to put a fence around them, the carrots are for the rabbits, who will eat them before you can. If you don't plant the carrot seeds, and instead you leave them on top of the ground, they are for the birds. 😂
Summer: Willie, you are right about how to plant seeds, make them grow into plants, and how to protect your plants from hungry animals. Rabbits love carrots as much as we do, and birds love seeds. Baby G, that idiom, "for the birds", means something is worthless. If something is for the birds, it is not good, and shouldn't be taken seriously. It is stupid and is not important.
Baby G: What are idioms?
Summer: Idioms are groups of words, which together mean something totally different than the individual words do. You can't use the words in the idiom to figure out what the idiom means. For example, the idiom, "it is raining cats and dogs", means it is raining very hard, and there is a lot of wind, not that cats and dogs are literally falling out of the sky like rain. If you "feel a bit under the weather", you feel a little sick. You aren't actually under the weather. Remember, weather is the state of the sky. It is sunny, cloudy, raining, snowing, etc. There are lots of other idioms.
Baby G: Are there any other bird idioms?
Summer: There are lots of those too. A "night owl" is someone who stays up late or does things late at night. An owl is a bird with big eyes that hunts at night for its food.

Willie: If a goose sees a big carrot, its eyes get big. It takes a gander at that carrot. What's good for the goose is good for the gander. 😂

Summer: Willie, a gander is a male goose. That idiom, "what's good for the goose is good for the gander" means something is good for both of them. Baby, a gander is also a look or a glance at something.

Baby G: What is a goose?

Summer: A goose is a waterbird with a long, flexible neck. A gooseneck is a pipe, or other object, that is curved like a goose's neck. An "ugly duckling" is an ugly child that grows up to be beautiful, or good looking, like a swan. A duckling is a baby duck. A duck is a waterbird with a short neck. A swan is a beautiful waterbird with a long neck.

Willie: I believe long necked giraffes are more beautiful than short necked ones. I would chicken out of being with a short necked one. 😂

Summer: Willie! There are no short-necked giraffes! Don't be scared of something that doesn't exist. Baby, when you "chicken out" of doing something, you back out of it, you don't do it, because you are scared. Chickens are birds too. "Birds of a feather flock together" means similar people, or people who like the same things, or people who are doing the same things, will be found together. All birds have feathers. A flock is a group of sheep, goats, or birds of one kind. The flock keeps, feeds, and travels together. A flock is also a large group of people. There are many more bird idioms. You can search online for them. Today is May 4. It is Bird Day. You can learn more about birds by researching them.

Baby G: World, today is Bird Day. Let's research together and learn about birds and bird idioms!

Baby G: Mama, what is Cinco De Mayo?

Willie: You have a kitchen sink full of mayonnaise. It is a sink o' the mayo party. You serve sandwiches with, count them, five kinds of meat, four kinds of cheese, three kinds of vegetables, two kinds of mustard, and one kind of mayo on them. They have everything thrown in, except the kitchen sink. 😂

Summer: Willie, giraffes don't eat meat, cheese, mustard, or mayo! And that saying, "everything but the kitchen sink", doesn't refer to a sink full of mayonnaise! Baby G, if you use "everything but the kitchen sink" when you do something, you use everything imaginable to do it. You use a much larger number of things than is necessary to do it. If you are going on a trip, and you pack everything but the kitchen sink, you are packing too many clothes, or packing too many things. You are bringing a lot of stuff, whether you'll need it or not. Cinco De Mayo is Spanish for Five of May. Today is May 5. On Cinco De Mayo, people in Mexico celebrate something that happened there. People in the USA just like to have a party and eat Mexican food.

Baby G: What is Mexican food?

Summer: It is things like tacos, tostadas, burritos, enchiladas, etc. It may contain a lot of tortillas, meat, poultry, or fish, cheese, beans, and vegetables. It may be topped with salsa, sour cream, or guacamole made from avocados.

Willie: Last year, your mama got a carrot taco. Everyone watching the live cam saw that. This time, will our human family remember to bring a carrot taco for me? I am so deprived! 😂

Summer: Willie! You are not deprived! People watching the live cam cannot see everything. They don't see much of your pen. They see my private feeder, but not yours. They assume our shared feeder is your only source of hay and accuse me of taking more than my fair share. They also assume that you don't get treats, because they see us get them, and don't see you get any, but that is not true. You have your own separate feeder that is out of view, the live cam does not show it to viewers. Our human family treats you too. You are just as important to this family, to our human family, and to our viewers, as we are. Baby, in English, you count, one, two, three, four, and five. In Spanish, you count uno, dos, tres, cuatro, and cinco.

Willie: He barely knows English, and how to count! Why are you confusing him by teaching him Spanish, a language of love? Instead, you should teach him the language of giraffe love. It is easy to learn. There aren't any words. 😂

Summer: Willie, Spanish is a Romance language. Some other Romance languages are Portuguese, French, Italian and Romanian. Baby, the primary language in the USA is English. It is the one most people use. If you can't speak English, when you tell a doctor what is wrong, he may know your language, or he may not. He might not be able to help you. If you work with other people, they may not understand you. The work might not get done. Everyone in the USA needs to learn English, so they can understand each other. But once you know English, learning other languages is a good thing. So is learning about the history and culture of other countries, such as Mexico.

Baby G: World, today is Cinco De Mayo. Let's have a party, eat Mexican food, learn another language, and learn some history. Those are all good things.

Baby G: Mama, what is a Penny Dreadful?
Willie: I dread your many questions. I dread them even more if they are repeats. You already asked about pennies. Now, you are asking a dreaded, repeat penny question, a "penny, dreadful".
Summer: Willie, earlier he asked about cents, which are pennies. A Penny Dreadful is not a penny, and today's question is not a repeat! Baby G, a Penny Dreadful was a cheap, sensational comic or storybook about adventure, crime or violence. It was divided into parts. Each part was sold in the UK for a penny. Some people, those who loved reading the Penny Dreadfuls, or who couldn't afford regular books, looked forward to buying the next installment, the next part of the story, each week. Other people, those who wrote, or sold, or bought regular books, hated the Penny Dreadfuls. Those people said they were dreadful, horrible, awful books.
Baby G: What is a comic?
Willie: I am a comic. Lessons can be boring. Today is Sunday. Sunday lessons are especially boring. If I am funny, you can laugh with me. If I am not, you can laugh at me. Either way, you will get some laughs. You need some laughs every day, not just on Sundays, or while in class.
Summer: Willie, you are a stand-up comic, or comedian. You are right, laughter helps when learning about things. But every class comedian needs to know when to be quiet, and not interfere with the lesson. Baby, comics are also cartoons or illustrated stories, with very few words. The pictures tell you the story. There may be speech balloons, telling you what people in the comic are saying. There may be thought bubbles, telling you what people or animals are thinking. Words in a narrative box may describe what is happening now, or what happened before now. They may tell you the setting for the story, where or when it occurred, or why the characters in the story are there. Comics are often funny, but they don't have to be. The ones that make you laugh often show up in a Sunday newspaper, or in a magazine. Today is World Laughter Day.
Baby G: Were other things sold for a penny?
Summer: Yes. The Penny Black was the world's first postage stamp that came with its own adhesive, its own glue. Today is May 6. The

Penny Black was first used on May 6, 1840. Penny candy was what it sounds like, candy that was sold for a penny.

Baby G: Are there other sayings or idioms that are about pennies?

Summer: Just like our penny is part of our dollar, the UK has a penny that is part of their pound. The saying, "penny-wise and pound-foolish", means you are very careful about the small stuff, the pennies, and wasteful, or not careful, with the big stuff, the pounds. "In for a penny, in for a pound" means you commit yourself to finishing what you start, no matter how much time, effort, or money it takes to do it. That is true, even if it turns out to be harder to do than you expected. A "penny for your thoughts" means I want to know what you are thinking. If I give you my "two cents worth", I am telling you what I think, without you asking me.

Willie: She'll give you her two scents worth, but you will have to ask her for them by swinging your neck and bumping her. They are milk and ... 😂

Summer: Willie! Don't finish that sentence! He is still too young to learn about that! Besides, he will get that from his future mate, not me. He will be weaned soon and won't even get milk from me.

Baby G: World, today is World Laughter Day. Let's enjoy some laughs while we learn about things.

Baby G: Mama, what does it mean to reach the end of the road?
Summer: Baby G, when you reach the end of the road, you can go no further. The end of the road is the moment when someone or something cannot get better, or someone dies. It is also the final step or conclusion of something. It is done.
Willie: Finding out if there are any carrots at the end of the rainbow is too hard. It is a hard road. It takes too much time and energy. I will give up and conclude there are no carrots there. I need to stop now and beg for carrots on the side of the road, or I will die of hunger. I will reach the end of my own road, before I will reach the end of the real road. 😂
Summer: Willie, just because you haven't found carrots at the end of the rainbow, or at the end of the road, that doesn't mean there are none. Don't give up your dreams, just because of a hard road. You have plenty of food here, which you can take on the road. Then you can pursue your dreams. Meanwhile, you won't die from hunger! Baby, a real road goes a little way, then it does one of five things: The road crosses another road, the intersection or crossroads looks like a plus sign +, and both roads keep going; the road forks, and becomes two new roads, the fork looks like a Y, and the new roads keep going; the road merges with another road, and both roads are replaced by a new road, it looks like an upside down Y, and the new road keeps going; the road touches another road, the intersection looks like a T, and the first road ends, but the other road keeps going; or the road just ends, and there is land or water beyond the end. The road may end in a circle, a cul-de-sac. It looks like a lollipop. If the road just ends abruptly, it is called a dead end. When roads cross or fork, you have a decision to make: Which road will you take? You will have more company on the road when roads merge. When a road ends, there is no way to keep going on it. You have reached the end of the road.
Willie: If your road is made of rope, which do you reach first, the end of your rope, or the end of the road? 😂
Summer: Willie, roads are made of stones, gravel, asphalt, concrete, dirt, etc., not rope! There are some rope bridges that are partly made

from rope or cables. Baby, when you reach the end of your rope, you are so frustrated, or so annoyed, you can't stand it. You have no more patience or strength, you are exhausted.

Baby G: Has my journey reached the end of the road?

Summer: Oh no. Your journey continues. You may reach the end of one road, one stage of your life, but you will start another. Already, you have learned so much, and shared so many wonderful things with the world. But there are many more amazing things to discover.

Willie: It is amazing to me that you eat almost as much as we do now, but your mama still hasn't weaned you! It is really amazing that our human family hasn't realized that they need to put more hay in our shared feeder. We are eating for three now! 😂

Summer: Willie, it is amazing to me that, after telling you many times that you get plenty of food in your own private feeder, and the hay in the shared feeder is just extra food for snacks, it never sinks into your head! Baby, you will learn and do many more things, and go down many roads during your lifetime. The world still wants to join you on your journey. It still wants to learn with you and learn from you.

Baby G: World, already we have shared so many wonderful things, and learned so much. But we are not done, our journey continues!

The End.

Printed in Great Britain
by Amazon